THE **MENACERS**

DONALD HAMILTON

A *MATT HELM* NOVEL

THE MENACERS

TITAN BOOKS

The Menacers
Print edition ISBN: 9781783292929
E-book edition ISBN: 9781783292936

Published by Titan Books
A division of Titan Publishing Group Ltd
144 Southwark Street, London SE1 0UP

First edition: August 2014
1 2 3 4 5 6 7 8 9 10

A CIP catalogue record for this title is available from the British Library.

Printed and bound in the United States.

Did you enjoy this book? We love to hear from our readers.
Please email us at readerfeedback@titanemail.com or write to us at
Reader Feedback at the above address.

To receive advance information, news, competitions, and exclusive
offers online, please sign up for the Titan newsletter on our website:
www.titanbooks.com

THE **MENACERS**

1

I always feel a little bad about smuggling a firearm through Mexican customs. The boys in khaki make their inspection so nice and casual you feel you're taking advantage of their courtesy. Of course, if you're found in their country later with an unregistered gun, particularly a revolver or pistol, and most particularly a big .45 auto—the Mexican Army caliber—they'll throw you in jail and lose the key, but that's a chance you take in a good many countries with much less violent histories than Mexico.

Mine wasn't a .45, just a little .38 Special, and it was pretty well hidden in a compartment designed for the purpose, so I wasn't really worried when the man approached my suitcase. I needn't have given it a thought. He saw that I stood innocently ready with the key, so he didn't even make me open it. He just hefted it briefly to determine, perhaps, if I was packing any large gold ingots or weight-lifting equipment. A moment later my bag was on its way out to the plane on the ramp.

I had to wait half an hour longer, with a lot of other people, before they'd let me aboard. The Juarez terminal building isn't air-conditioned; however, Mexican beer is very cooling and it was good to be working again after spending most of the summer at the goddamn ranch.

The goddamn ranch—we hardly ever call it just the ranch—is located in Arizona, which is no place to be in summer. But even with ideal weather, the goddamn ranch is no place to be. It's where we're sent when somebody decides a thorough mental and physical overhaul is required. I wasn't really in bad shape, but I had collected a scar or two, and perhaps a disturbing memory or two, since the last time they'd checked me out, and that spring there was apparently nowhere in the world that my talents were needed for the moment, so I was shipped to Arizona for a good going-over.

I'd finally managed to get myself sprung by claiming urgent personal business in nearby Santa Fe, New Mexico—well, it's only some five hundred miles away—but not before I'd been given the works in every department from psychiatry to marksmanship. I was so damn healthy and efficient and dangerous I could hardly stand myself. I'd been in Santa Fe, where I'd lived in a previous incarnation, trying to tear myself down a bit at the local bistros with the help of an attractive acquaintance of many years' standing—named Carol, if you must know—when word had come through, never mind how, that I should transport myself to Mexico City immediately by the most direct and rapid method available.

This happened to be, to start with, a small commercial prop plane that fluttered down to El Paso in an erratic manner, touching earth here and there on the way. From the El Paso airport an eager taxi driver had rushed me south across the border into Juarez and halfway through Mexico, it seemed, before he caught up with the elusive Juarez airport somewhere far south of that city and collected his seven bucks fare.

He could have saved some of his Stirling-Moss-type efforts. I had time to spare, plenty of time in which to show my passport to the Mexican immigration man and receive my tourist card from him, and to smile at the nice customs official who passed my suitcase containing the little Smith & Wesson revolver and some other gear that he'd probably have found interesting, had he come across it…

The Aeronaves de Mexico plane also had a few stops to make, so we didn't reach Mexico City until well after dark. I got into a taxi with some other people—they have kind of communal airport cabs down there—and gave the name of the hotel at which I'd been instructed to stay. The driver wasn't sure he'd ever heard of a hostelry called the Monte Carlo, but I had the address, and he finally managed to get himself going the right way on a narrow, dark, grubby one-way street in an older part of town. He pulled up dubiously before a tremendous, dark, shabby doorway above which burned a small illuminated sign with the right name on it.

Well, it's only in the movies that a man in my profession gets to spend all his time in the best hotels surrounded by the most beautiful girls. I retrieved my suitcase, gave the man some U.S. currency since I didn't have any pesos, and approached the great doors cautiously. I mean, I supposedly had the word straight from Washington, but codes have been compromised before. There are, unfortunately, a few people in the world who don't like me, and one of them could be in Mexico, D.F.—which is what they call their capital city, the equivalent of our Washington, D.C.

It was, in other words, a good place for a trap, but nothing happened when I stepped inside. I just found myself in the spacious lobby of what had once, obviously, been a magnificent luxury hotel, now grown rather old and tired. A polite individual in a neat dark suit came around the desk to introduce himself as the manager and to ask, in perfect English, if I was Mr. Helm, Mr. Matthew Helm, who had a reservation.

When I said I was, he had a boy relieve me of my bag, and personally escorted me up a great marble staircase guarded by a fine brass railing that was nicely polished but didn't look as if, after all these years, it would bear a great deal of weight. He established me in a room with a ceiling at least fifteen feet high and made me promise that, if anything was needed for my comfort, I would call him at once.

After he'd departed, taking the bellboy with him, I looked around my quarters. I decided that I liked the place. It wasn't just another nylon-carpeted cell in another chrome-plated beehive. It had character. It also had clean sheets on the beds, and a full complement of working plumbing in the bathroom, including that practical European gadget known as a bidet. I was inspecting this curiosity when the telephone rang. I went back into the bedroom and picked it up.

"Señor Helm?" said an accented voice in my ear.

"This is Helm," I said.

"You seem to be in the clear so far," the voice said. "Nobody's tailing you that we can see. How do you like your accommodations? Very picturesque, don't you think, *amigo*? Hah! These people with their urgent missions, they expect one to perform instant housing miracles in the middle of the tourist season! Anyway, in that grand old place you can probably trust your phone; nobody'd bother to bug it since nobody stays there any more. I have a call for you. Just a minute." There was a silence as the relay man worked on the connection. He was a man I would probably never see, and if I saw him I wouldn't know him, and that was the way he liked it. His voice reached me again, speaking to someone else: "I have Helm on the line now. Go ahead, sir."

"Eric?" said a faraway man whose voice I recognized, using my code name, as was his custom. At least I thought he was far away. I figured he was probably calling from Washington, but of course he could have been right around the corner, modern communications being what they are.

"Eric here, sir," I said, and we went through some mandatory secret-agent stuff to satisfy the rulebook.

Mac said, "You have a reservation on Mexicana Airlines Flight 906 leaving at eight-twenty tomorrow morning for Guadalajara, Puerto Vallarta, Mazatlán, Guaymas, and Los Angeles. You will get off at Mazatlán, which is, I believe, a west coast port, beach resort, and sport-fishing center, of some seventy-five thousand people. An agent will make preliminary contact with you at the airport. You will check into the Hotel Playa Mazatlán, about three miles north of town, and behave like a vacationing tourist until she gets in touch with you again."

"She?" I said.

"Your contact is female, brunette, under thirty, and not unattractive, I'm informed. She is going under the name— it may be her own—of Priscilla Decker. She will be wearing white linen trousers, a flowered silk blouse, dark glasses, and one of those crazy palm-leaf hats that are sold on the beach. The adjective is not mine. I thought female trousers were not approved for public wear in Mexico."

"They aren't," I said, "and hooray for the Mexicans. But a lot of U.S. tourists couldn't care less if they offend the backward natives."

Mac said, "You have been described to the lady. When she sees you, she will remove her glasses and clean them briefly to give you the privilege of looking at her face. You will mop your forehead with your handkerchief as you pass."

"You're sure I shouldn't carry a red hibiscus in my teeth, sir? And simultaneously whistle a few bars of 'La Cucaracha,' just to show I can do it?"

Mac said gently, "As you will gather, this is a cooperative venture. The lady is not one of ours, nor is the man with whom she is working. We must follow the wishes of their department in the matter of identification. Just be sure you can recognize her. And don't be surprised if there's a bit of hostility. Nobody likes to be superseded on a job."

"I'm taking over from her?"

"You are taking over one phase of the operation from her and her male partner."

"And the nature of the operation, sir?"

"This, we are informed, does not concern us. We are to concentrate on our assigned duties."

"Which are?"

"There is someone to be brought out of Mexico; someone with certain information. An interview has already been taped, and the tape is safely in our hands, but some people at Los Alamos would like to check further, by direct interrogation."

"So it's a simple escort job on the face of it." I frowned at the wall of the room. "What's so tough about it that we were called in, and what are the boys on The Hill up to now, and who's the character they want to talk to, a stray scientist of some kind?"

"You ask too many questions, Eric." Mac's voice was mild. "I repeat, the nature of the Los Alamos project, by official decree, does not concern us."

"Yes, sir," I said. "Sorry, sir."

"I can tell you, however," Mac went on, "that the

subject of your assignment is not a scientist, just an individual named O'Leary who happens to have witnessed a phenomenon of interest to a special research team that has established temporary headquarters at Los Alamos. I should mention that for various reasons friend O'Leary is not eager to make the journey."

"That's nice," I said. "That helps."

"I should also add that other people from other parts of the world are apparently interested in the phenomenon observed by this O'Leary, extremely interested, to the extent of being willing to spend large sums of money, and perhaps a few lives, to obtain a detailed description."

"Yes, sir," I said. "And that's where I come in, to protect this valuable specimen of humanity? Body-guarding is hardly my specialty, sir."

"And protection isn't exactly what we have in mind, Eric. The people already on the job would probably serve quite well as protectors."

"I see," I said slowly. "That is, I think I see. But perhaps you'd better be a little more explicit."

"You may run into difficulties, bringing the subject north," Mac said. "And if difficulties should arise, serious difficulties, some people here in Washington want to be quite certain the matter is in the hands of an experienced operator who knows the proper steps to take and will not hesitate to take them." He was silent briefly, and went on: "There is a great deal of sentimentality in the world, Eric, but there is no place for it in our work."

"No, sir."

"I hope you understand the situation. We have the tape containing the essential data. Nobody else has it; we do. The Los Alamos team would like to check the information and perhaps elicit a few more details, but this is not absolutely necessary. What is necessary is that the information must be communicated to nobody else. No matter what has to be done to prevent it, this O'Leary person must not fall into other hands. Do I make myself perfectly clear?"

"No matter what has to be done," I repeated, making a face at the phone. "Yes, sir. It's clear. Is there anything else I should know?"

"Nothing that Miss Decker can't tell you. However, you are to keep in mind that our relations with our neighbors to the south have been deteriorating of late, to the extent that there is growing concern about the situation here in Washington. It is felt that a deliberate campaign of alienation is being waged by someone with considerable resources."

I said, "That's not exactly new. The communists have been playing their Yankee-go-home records all over Latin America for years."

"There are indications that their efforts have been intensified recently. So it would be well if you were careful not to give the anti-American propaganda machine anything to feed on."

I said sourly, "Sure. I'm to sneak into a foreign country with an illegal weapon, perform an illegal abduction—maybe even an illegal homicide—but I'm to be careful not to hurt anybody's feelings while I'm doing it. Yes, sir. Anything else, sir?"

Mac paid no attention to my sarcasm. "Nothing else, Eric," he said. "Well, just one more thing…"

"Yes, sir," I said, when he hesitated uncharacteristically.

He was silent a moment longer, then he asked abruptly: "Eric, do you believe in flying saucers?"

I was proud of my presence of mind. I didn't hesitate. "Yes, sir," I said.

"What?"

"I said 'Yes, sir.' Sir." It isn't often one has an advantage over him, and I rode it for what it was worth. "I saw one once, sir."

"Indeed? Where?"

"In Santa Fe, New Mexico, where I was living as a solid citizen in that happy period when I was out of your clutches for several years, sir, before you caught up with me again and shanghaied me back into service."

"As I recall, a great deal of duress was not required. What did you see?"

"A luminous, pulsating, greenish object moving steadily over town in a southeasterly direction, just about dusk. I saw it, and so did my former wife—she was still Mrs. Helm at the time—and so did another couple that was in the car with us. We all got out to make sure we weren't just getting reflections off the glass. We watched it until it kind of switched itself off and vanished, up near the mountains. When we got home, a few minutes later, I called the police. The officer who answered asked me politely to wait a moment as he was just taking down another report of the same nature."

"Other people confirmed the sighting?"

"All the way across town. It was in the newspaper the next day. You can check the files if you wish. I think it was some time in fifty-eight or fifty-nine." I stopped, but he did not speak. I said, "I don't claim to have seen an extra-terrestrial space ship crewed by little men with pointed heads, but *something* flew over the city, and it wasn't any type of aircraft with which I'm familiar."

"Indeed?" He didn't sound convinced. "That's very interesting, Eric."

"Yes, sir. Of course the Air Force continues to insist there's nothing up there. Well, it was a hell of a lifelike hallucination, shared by a hell of a lot of people. It makes one kind of wonder just what the fly-boys are trying to cover up." I paused. "Anything else?"

"No." His voice was curt. I had a hunch he'd had a pep talk ready for me, but I'd made the wrong answer and aborted his little speech on keeping an open mind about strange manifestations no matter how incredible. At least I figured that was the subject he'd had in mind, and I knew he didn't like to have his speeches go to waste. Or maybe he just disapproved of my doubting attitude towards the U.S.A.F. He went on in businesslike tones: "Just remember the instructions. Alive, the subject goes nowhere but Los Alamos. This is the preferable solution. The other is, however, perfectly acceptable. Oh, and Eric…"

"Yes, sir."

"Try to complete this mission within a reasonable time. It is only a favor we are doing to certain people in Washington, who want to make sure the matter is in competent hands. I have another assignment for you, or will have, as soon as I can find you an adequate partner. Unfortunately, young ladies of character and mentality suitable for our type of work seem to be in short supply lately, and our trained people are all engaged elsewhere."

I said, "Yes, sir. If I stumble over a sufficiently bloodthirsty chick, I'll let you know."

I hung up and sat there for a little, thinking about flying saucers, for God's sake.

2

In the morning, I had a taxi run me out to the airport early enough for me to have breakfast in the glass-walled restaurant overlooking the field. It had no particular character. It looked like any glossy airport restaurant anywhere in the world.

When I got back down to the Mexicana desk, where they were just starting to check in my flight, I discovered something that might have come as a traumatic shock to a younger and less hardened member of the organization: I learned that Mac wasn't quite omniscient and infallible. At least he didn't know Mexican airlines. What I mean is, I had no reservation. Whatever passenger list he'd had my name put on somewhere, that particular list hadn't got here.

The young man behind the counter studied all his documents and manifests and records and shook his head. He went into the office and came out shaking his head some more. We held a consultation, and he assured me he would get me on the plane somehow. I showed him the corner of a fifty-peso note I'd taken in change at the hotel. He grinned.

"You will catch your plane, señor," he said, looking me straight in the eye, "you will catch it, and it will cost you nothing extra."

So much for the prevalent theory that everybody in that country has his hand out. Chastened, I stood and waited beside my suitcase until, at eight o'clock, the deadline for no-shows, he waved me forward and checked me through. We took off, and would have had a good view of the high valley in which the Mexican capital lies, the cradle of the old Aztec civilization, if it hadn't been for the new Los-Angeles-type mist. If they haven't got a real smog problem yet, there in the Distrito Federal, they soon will have.

At Guadalajara, we were booted out of the plane for twenty minutes, after which we climbed over some pretty spectacular mountains and glided down to the coast and Puerto Vallarta, a pretty little seaport, where we had to deplane again, as the jargon goes. They don't let you stay aboard their aircraft while they're brushing and currying it between runs.

I'd been pretty relaxed so far, enjoying the ride and the scenery, but now as we got back into our seats and were flown up the green Pacific coastline towards Mazatlán, which means the place of the deer, I felt the familiar, nervous, beginning-of-the-job tightness take hold of my throat and abdomen. It's a sensation you never lose, no matter how long you stay in the business. At least I don't seem to.

Not only was I working again after several months' layoff, but I was working with people who were bound to resent me, which meant I couldn't trust them even to make it to the john without explicit instructions and careful supervision…

My contact was there, all right, in the Mazatlán terminal, in her snug white linen pants and her crazy palm-leaf hat. She wasn't exactly what I'd expected. She looked like a kid. I don't mean the cuddly, blonde, lisping, baby-face type, but the slim, dark, big-eyed, hollow-cheeked kind of young girl who doesn't seem aware of the fact that she's going to be beautiful some day.

She annoyed me at first glance, which wasn't quite fair, since I'd been prejudiced against her before I ever saw her. But now I wasn't condemning her merely for her taste in clothes and countersigns. The two most dangerous aberrations in our line of work are idealism and innocence, and if I was any judge she suffered from both.

She was talking to a tanned, rather husky young woman with short blonde hair who wore a skimpy, sleeveless, bright orange garment with native designs on it—just a sack with holes for the arms and head—undoubtedly purchased at one of the local tourist shops. My girl took off her sunglasses casually and wiped them with a Kleenex as the crowd from the plane kind of washed me past her.

I responded by mopping my face with a handkerchief as instructed. It wasn't hard to make the gesture convincing. I was dressed for Santa Fe and Mexico City, mountain communities a mile and a half high, cool and dry. Down here at sea level the temperature was in the high nineties and the humidity was running it a close race for the hundred mark.

I did notice, as I went past, that Priscilla Decker didn't look quite as dewy at short range as she had across the room. She was getting on towards twenty-five, I judged, and she was beginning to show just a hint of the dried-up look of the professional virgin, which is what happens to them if they're left on the vine instead of being picked, so to speak, at the proper time. I didn't know whether this was good or bad from my point of view, but at least I wouldn't have to make allowances for extreme youth. She'd had the years. If she hadn't taken advantage of them, that wasn't my fault.

That was all there was to it. I didn't look to see where she went; I wasn't supposed to pay her any attention. She was supposed to find me when the time came. I waited for my suitcase to be unloaded—I don't think flying is going to be really practical until they invent self-propelled luggage to match the planes—and was driven to the Hotel Playa by a genial robber who charged me twenty pesos, about a dollar sixty, which was obviously too much since he was disappointed when I didn't give him an argument. There was a reservation waiting for me here, but it didn't really matter. The winter season wouldn't begin for a month or so yet, and they had lots of room.

Playa means beach in Spanish, and they were situated

right on theirs. It seemed like a hell of a good idea, so after making sure the air-conditioner was going full blast in my room, I changed into trunks and walked out there. Some pretty big waves were breaking against the shore— well, big for a calm summer day—but I'd recently learned a bit about surf and swimming in the line of duty, and I watched the crests briefly to get the timing, and dove under one and paddled out a ways, ducking beneath the white stuff as it came at me.

There were some other people playing around out there, including a woman in a white satin bathing suit—a sleek, one-piece job, not a bikini—who caught my eye for some reason, perhaps just because I have that kind of an eye and she was the only woman venturing out that far. She swam pretty well, but with a European touch to her style that I couldn't quite identify. Maybe she behaved just a bit as if she'd been brought up on the breast stroke and the crawl were a later accomplishment.

She was quite slender, almost thin, and her hard adult body sheathed in wet white satin was a lot sexier than most of this soft nymphet stuff you see on the beach covered by practically nothing but a good tan. Something about her had aroused my curiosity—if you want to call it curiosity—so when she headed towards shore I gave her a minute or so and then picked up a crest, paddled hard to match its speed, and let it carry me in.

A good-sized breaking wave, even a summer wave, can give you a pretty rough ride; it's kind of like being shaken by an angry dog. I cut out of it before it buried my head in the sand, and stood up. I'd been carried past the woman, and I turned casually to seaward as I pounded the water out of my ears, and there she was, coming towards me, smiling faintly.

"I wondered how long it would take you to recognize me, Matthew," she said.

For a moment I still wasn't quite sure. I mean, the lady whose name popped into my mind had been pretty good at changing her appearance to suit the job, but she'd always been a fairly well-developed specimen of womanhood. She'd often been described as sexy in official reports— sometimes even as voluptuous—but never as slender. But it was Vadya, all right. There was no doubt about it. I'd slept with her a couple of times and shot her once; I ought to know.

I said, "I'm ashamed of you, Vadya, trying to fool your old friends like that. When did you decide to go on a diet?"

"Diet, hell," she said, "if you'll excuse it, darling. Do you know how many operations they had to make after you were so ungentlemanly as to put a bullet into me, and how many operations to erase the signs of those operations? I was a shadow, a skeleton, when they finished carving me up and putting me back together. And then it seemed like a good idea to try to keep my new svelte figure. Some people do not have as sharp eyes as others. Obviously. I have been here for several days. If anyone among your people had recognized this sylph-like creature as Vadya, you would not have been sent here, would you? They would have sent someone I did not know, instead."

"You knew I was coming?"

"Of course not. We did not know who was coming; but we knew someone else probably would be, besides those already here. It is not a job for a college boy with a degree in accounting or foreign relations, even if he can draw his pistol in a fraction of a second and make magnificent scores on the targets that look like men but are really paper. Nor is it a job for an unclaimed maiden with beautiful ideals and strange yearnings." Vadya smiled. "It is a job for crude, realistic people like you and me, darling. Of course, now that you are here, I will probably have to kill you, but I am glad to see you nevertheless. Let us get out of these soapsuds and have a drink."

3

Some people have a thing about fraternizing with the enemy. They seem to feel that disloyalty is something you can catch across a table, like the common cold. They act as if the only safe way to remain faithful to duty and country is to quarantine yourself with none but certified patriots in a place where no sinister bacteria of subversion can possibly reach you from the infected creeps on the other side.

Personally, I have a little more faith in my loyalty than this, and if the enemy wants to fraternize, I'm happy to be fraternized with. Why work like hell to ferret out someone's intentions by devious methods, when you can maybe get him, or her, to tell you all about them over a cold rum Collins?

As I settled down in a wooden chair under one of the numerous brown-thatched cabanas that sprouted like mushrooms from the sand in front of the hotel, sharing beach space with some green palms and a rustic life-guard tower, I reminded myself that Vadya undoubtedly had reasons of her own for renewing our old acquaintance. She hadn't picked the exact moment of my arrival to go gamboling in the surf for nothing. Well, that was all right. We'd played this game before, and while the score had been very close upon occasion, I was a little ahead on points. At least I'd never had to have any of her bullets dug out of me.

I sat back and sipped my drink and listened to the surf, therefore, waiting for her to break the silence first and set the conversational mood however she pleased. Far up the beach some kids were popping firecrackers. It's about the only thing I really have against the Mexicans. They don't wait for the local equivalent of the Fourth of July; they'll set the damn things off any time of the year, day or night—and in our business we tend to be kind of allergic to sudden loud noises.

Aside from the distant explosions, everything was very peaceful. A little spidery sand crab of some kind popped out of a hole not six feet away; a shore bird, perhaps a sandpiper, tripped along down where the sand was wet, daintily avoiding the waves that reached out for him. There were some islands off the point on which the hotel stood. Across the blue bay to the left was the city of Mazatlán, spread out along the shore.

It looked like a sizeable community. I remembered that Mac had credited it with a population of seventy-five thousand. Clouds hung around the horizon as a reminder that this was the tail end of the rainy season down here, but the rest of the sky was blue and the sun was bright.

Vadya stirred and reached out to pat my hand lightly, and the sand crab, if that's what it was, scuttled back into its miniature den.

"Darling," Vadya said, "it *is* nice to see you again, even if you did almost kill me."

I said, "That'll teach you. When you slip a guy a Mickey, don't stand around waiting to see him fall on his face. He might just manage to get out a gun and shoot you first."

"I guess I was fatuous to expect an apology." Her voice was a trifle sharp. "Or even an expression of regret."

I grinned. "Cut it out. Under similar circumstances, you'd have done exactly the same thing to me, if I'd been dumb enough to let you. You might even have shot straighter than I did." This wasn't getting us anywhere, and I asked, "Who's handling the main job for you here, or is it a big secret?"

It was a crude, head-on approach, and she stalled automatically: "Why, I am handling the job. The whole job. Why should I need anybody else?"

I said, "Because it's not your type of job and you know it. You're just running interference, I figure. You're here to make with the sex, and the guns if necessary; to take me out of play at the proper time—me, or whoever was sent. For the heavy work, the primary objective, they'd have somebody else lined up, somebody with more muscle and less finesse. Who is it?"

"Do you really expect me to tell you?"

"Sure," I said. "Why be cagey about something I'm bound to find out pretty soon, anyway?"

Vadya shrugged. "All right. If you must know, Harsek is coming. I was handy, vacationing in Acapulco. I was just rushed up here to keep track of the subject until Harsek arrives."

I whistled softly. "Harsek, eh? The Mad Czech?"

"He is not so mad. He is just very, very tough. Tougher than you are, darling."

"Nobody's tougher than me," I said, grinning. "Except perhaps you. Certainly not a fat bully-boy with a shaved head who's made his reputation scaring poor little Turks and Arabs with his silly Luger. A Luger, for Christ's sake! A story-book pistol with a trigger pull that works around fifteen corners before it gets to where the gun goes off; a muzzle-light cannon that shakes like a leaf in the breeze. I never knew a Luger boy yet who wasn't strictly for show."

Vadya laughed. "You are just talking to make yourself brave."

"Who needs courage against Harsek?" I asked flamboyantly. "All I'll need is a fly-swatter. There'll be nothing left but a spot of grease. When is he coming?"

"I have told you all I'm going to," she said, smiling. "And you have given me nothing in return but boasts and ballistics."

"Harsek," I said thoughtfully. "I thought he functioned strictly in the Near East. They must want whatever we've got—or whoever we've got—pretty badly to pry Harsek loose from his favorite stamping grounds and send him all the way over here. How much manpower does he plan to use?"

"Really, darling! You want a great deal of information in exchange for none at all."

"Exchange?" I said. "Why, I thought we were just having a pleasant chat. Two old friends—well, enemies — meeting again after so many months. You make it sound like bargaining day at the local *mercado*. What do you want to know?" She didn't answer at once. I watched a white seabird commit apparent suicide out there, hurling itself deliberately into the waves. A moment later it was airborne again, presumably with something in its beak or claws, but that was a detail I couldn't make out at the distance. Of course, it could have missed its target. This happens, even among birds. I said, casually, "It's a screwball deal, isn't it?"

"What is?" Vadya's voice had a cautious sound.

"A bunch of grown people getting all stirred up about some kook's psychedelic visions." Regardless of my own beliefs, I had a hunch that a skeptical attitude would be more profitable here. I asked, "What's Spanish for flying saucer, anyway?"

She glanced at me warily. "*Plato volante*, I believe," she said. "Or *disco volante*. Why?"

I grinned at her. "All right, play it close to the chest if you like. But I must say I'm starting to wonder about those guys in Washington. I've had a lot of weirdies sprung on me in the way of assignments, but this is the first time they've put me to chasing imaginary spacecraft, or even the screwball who imagined them."

She permitted herself a small laugh. "Yes, it is rather

lurid, is it not? I must say I had the same feeling when the mission was explained to me." She moved her bare shoulders ruefully. "Of course, one asks no questions. One has one's orders."

She wasn't giving much away, not even her true feelings on the subject—but at least the UFO gambit hadn't come as a total surprise to her. Whatever wild notions were going around, they apparently weren't confined to Washington.

"That's right," I said. "One does."

"Well, how are you going to obey yours, darling? Now that you know with whom you have to deal. Do you really think you can get your prisoner past Harsek and me, and across the border into the United States?" She glanced at me. "What is your plan, darling? It must be very good."

I laughed. "Now we come to it. A straight question at last. Well, in return for Harsek's name, I'll give you a straight answer. Pay close attention, doll, because this is important."

"I am listening. Tell me what you plan to do to outwit us, two of the best agents in the business if I may flatter myself as well as Harsek. Tell me. Then maybe I will tell you if it will work."

"Outwit you, hell," I said. "Why should I bother? My orders are simple and straightforward. I have explicit instructions to shoot this character with the vivid imagination—to shoot him stone dead—if you or Harsek so much as crook a finger or lift a voice in his direction. What did you think they sent a guy like me down here for, baby, to make sure he got his two A.M. feeding on schedule?"

There was a little silence. Vadya was looking down at her glass so that I could not see her eyes, but I knew her pretty well, and I had an uneasy hunch that I'd just said something that amused her—and something that she'd wanted to hear, as well, although this did not really make sense, in the light of what I knew about the situation. Of course, I didn't know everything, and some of what I did know could be wrong.

Vadya raised her glass, and drained it. "I see," she said. "I wondered. This explains things."

I said, "Of course, your names weren't specifically mentioned in the orders, but the principle laid down was clear. I intend to follow it. And then I'll go back to Santa Fe, New Mexico, where I left a drink waiting—a drink and a lady named Carol—when I rushed off to chase little green men in the sky. The drink's probably warm by now, but liquor and ice are plentiful up there. The lady's another matter. She's kind of special, you might say unique. She was quite warm when I left her. I hope she hasn't cooled."

Vadya smiled. "You are trying to make me jealous. That's childish."

"Maybe."

"And also you are giving me a warning, are you not, Matt? One might even call it an ultimatum, mightn't one?"

"One might," I said. I still had the nagging feeling that I was playing into her hands somehow, but I'd already started on this heavy-menace routine and it was too late to switch to another approach. I made my voice hard. "Pass the word, doll. I'm not here to fool around, and guarding the body is not my sport. I flunked my Red Cross lifesaving course, but I did real well in Practical Pistolry. I am taking this imaginative specimen north alive if you leave me alone. But if you make one move, one half a move, all we'll have is a corpse to share—and don't try calling my bluff, doll, because it's not a bluff. My instructions are to consider this crackpot strictly expendable, and rather than lose him to you, or Harsek, I'll expend him right now." I got to my feet abruptly. "How do you sign for the drinks around here?"

"Take that chit to the bar." Vadya's voice was expressionless. "They'll give you a slip to fill out. Incidentally, there's a space for *propina*, which means tip, and fifteen percent seems to be customary."

I looked down at her for a moment, feeling baffled and uncomfortable, the way a man always feels in the presence of a woman who knows more than he does and is smart enough to take full advantage of her knowledge.

"Thanks," I said sourly. "I've only lived along the Mexican border for about half my life, but thanks anyway. It's nice to know what *propina* means after all these years."

Vadya shrugged. "You were so stupid about *disco volante*. I am aware that you know some Spanish—it's in the dossier—but I thought if that is the way you want to play it, I would oblige you. Matthew?"

"Yes?"

"I really bear no hard feelings for what you did to

me. And I really expected no apologies. You know that, don't you?"

"Sure," I said.

"We do not have to play tough and make faces at each other, do we? Will you take me to dinner? Seven-thirty in the lobby. We will go to the Copa de Leche, which means glass of milk, and is the closest thing to a first-class restaurant to be found in this town. It is air-conditioned, too. Seven-thirty is early for dinner in Mexico, very early, but you will be tired from all your traveling." She smiled up at me. "I am not luring you away from the action, darling. Nothing is planned for tonight. However, if you are suspicious and want to eat right here instead, that is all right, too. The food is quite passable and the dining room is up on that balcony and reasonably cool. But do wear a coat and tie in either case. One gets so tired of seeing grown men in romper suits, like superannuated schoolboys."

I grinned. "Seven-thirty. Coat and tie. Check."

I walked up the sand, leaving her there, and signed for the drinks in the bar that was a sort of half-open veranda adjoining the lobby. As I came past the desk afterwards, I caught a glimpse of Priscilla Decker watching me through the glass wall of the nearby souvenir shop. I went quickly in there and found her studying a rack of magazines, predominantly in English, and with a surprisingly large percentage of U.S. girlie publications, for a respectable hotel newsstand in a foreign land.

Well, the Mexican male really goes for this literature, I'm told; and if he doesn't, he can't afford to admit it. It is part of his image, part of what is known as the cult of *machismo*, or rampant maleness. He's supposed to be so damn virile he comes on like a bull at the mere sight of a female photographed in a mildly suggestive pose with a minimum of clothing. Personally, I prefer to save myself for real live women. I can't seem to get much satisfaction from photographs, but I guess it's all a matter of taste.

I saw my contact holding one of the magazines vaguely, only pretending to examine it. She put it back hastily, flushing pink, when she got around to actually looking at the bosomy lingerie lady on the cover.

"Tsk, tsk," I said in her ear. "That's man-stuff. What you want is a health magazine featuring a muscle-bound weight lifter flexing his oiled biceps. Where can we talk?"

"Go away!" she whispered urgently. "Go away! We're not supposed to be seen together. We haven't been authorized to break cover—"

I said, "For God's sake stop playing Sally Spy, girl agent. We've been made and you know it, so let's just skip the cute undercover stuff for the time being. Is that your key?" I took it from her fingers. "Room 116? Let's go."

4

It was a motel-style room entered directly from outdoors, pretty much like mine and, I suppose, like all the others in the place with the exception of a few larger suites or apartments. Two beds were arranged sofa-fashion along the left-hand wall, facing a closet, bathroom, and built-in dresser. A couple of chairs, a low cocktail table, and a luggage stand with a green vinyl suitcase on it, completed the list of furnishings.

There were doors and windows at both ends of the room. From the parking lot, you could walk right through to the beach—and see right through, too, if the curtains were pulled back. It wasn't an arrangement that made for a great deal of privacy if you had to leave things open and depend on the sea breeze for ventilation.

However, with the air-conditioner on, the doors and windows closed, and the draperies drawn, the outside world moved off into the remote distance. Even the usual hotel noises were pretty well masked by the soft hum of the cooling machinery. All that could really be heard from outside was the slow beat of the surf.

Priscilla Decker stopped inside the door and turned to face me, saying, "Well, Mr. Helm?"

I let her question, if that's what it was, hang in the air temporarily. I had other things, and people, to engage my attention. I looked first at the young man standing near the door by which we had entered, because he was holding a gun and aiming it at me.

Priscilla said, "It's all right, Tony... Mr. Helm, Tony Hartford."

It didn't seem like a very convincing name. It sounded like something somebody clever had put together, picking the Tony for youthful charm and the Hartford for confidence-inspiring respectability. Of course, there was no reason why it should be his real name, under the circumstances—just as there was no real reason why Priscilla Decker should be hers. Both could have been, and probably had been, picked to suit the characters they were playing.

I watched Tony put the gun away. His face didn't break into a smile of greeting, nor did his hand present itself eagerly for a warm handshake. Well, I could live without his friendship. He was what I'd classify as low-grade, pretty-boy help. To be specific, the guy was a lean, tanned, sulky young male specimen with long wavy brown hair that had blondish streaks in it put there either by the sun or by Tony himself with the aid of peroxide or whatever they use for the purpose nowadays. He was wearing very

close-fitting light slacks, and a knitted white sports shirt
hanging loose about his narrow hips.

One of these days, the House Un-American Activities
Committee is going to discover a significant sign of
communist penetration, hitherto overlooked by the
subversion experts. It used to be that the chief sartorial
difference between a Russian and the rest of humanity
was that the Russian wore his shirttail out. Now they've
got us all doing it, obviously a sinister plot against
American decency, neatness, and self-respect...

Having seen the gun safely stored away, I could afford
to look, at last, from Tony Hartford to the fourth person
in the room—which was where I'd really wanted to look
all the time. I understood, now, why Vadya had found
my conversation on the beach mildly amusing. She'd
obviously known, as I had not, that O'Leary was a lady.
At least the person watching me from the big chair by
the far window was a girl, and a redhaired girl at that—a
redhaired girl with a bandaged arm and a bruised cheek.

After the damage, the long, straight hair was what one
noticed first. It wasn't any of those sissy shades of reddish
gold they put into bottles nowadays and sell to blondes
and other interlopers. This was red hair the way red hair
used to be before the chemists got into the act: brick-red,
carrot-red, unmistakably genuine, since nobody would go
out deliberately and pick such a violent color to live with.

As is often the case with real redheads, as opposed to
the bottled variety, the girl was less striking than the hair.
One expected a truly spectacular female to go with the

fiery coiffure, but all there was was a slim, pale, faintly freckled young lady, wearing a short white skirt of the slick material called sharkskin, and a pale green jersey top that looked as if somebody had started out to make a turtle-necked sweater but had tired of the project before tackling the sleeves.

"Helm?" she said, giving me a hard look across the room. "So this is the sinister character we've all been waiting for!"

Priscilla said, "Mrs. Annette O'Leary, Mr. Matthew Helm."

Annette O'Leary pursed her lips thoughtfully, looking me up and down. When she spoke, it was with a deliberate country accent. "He's not much for wide, is he?" she said to nobody in particular, "but he's sure hell for tall." Her voice reverted to normal. "So this is the imported strong-arm man who's going to drag me back to the States whether I want to go or not! Where does he pack his little whip and gun?"

Nobody answered her. I asked, "If she's Mrs. O'Leary, who's Mr. O'Leary?"

There was a rather embarrassed silence from my two associates, so-called. It was the girl herself who answered: "If you must know, my husband, Jim O'Leary, died in Vietnam last year, being patriotic. It runs in the family, I guess. Look what I'm getting for being patriotic right here in Mexico!"

I grinned. "Is that what you're being, Mrs. O'Leary?"

The red-haired girl said angrily, "Well, I could have

kept quiet about what I saw out there on the water and stayed out of trouble, couldn't I? Or I could have sold it to somebody who was interested—that woman your friends, here, claim to be a communist agent—for quite a bit of money. Don't think the offer wasn't made, and don't think I can't use the stuff. But instead of cashing in on what I'd seen, I got in touch with the representatives of my native land, like a good little girl, and had them send somebody to take it all down on tape for free. So what happens? So I'm cooped up in a hotel room under guard for days, waiting for a high-powered secret agent type to either escort me north across the border against my will or, I suppose, kill me if I object."

She gave me a quick, questioning glance to see if she'd guessed right. I said, "Smart girl. I'm glad you realize that if you object, or if other people object, you're dead." I looked from her to Priscilla and her good-looking male partner—well, good-looking if you like that kind of looks. I said, "You heard, I hope. I don't know what instructions you've been operating under, but as of now, that's the official word. This lady goes to Los Alamos. She goes nowhere else in the world—at least not in this world. If anything happens, if the situation looks the least bit doubtful, put a bullet right between her eyes. Do I make myself clear?"

There was an embarrassed little silence, as if I'd said something vulgar or obscene. After a moment, Priscilla spoke in her prim way: "Well, it's your problem now, isn't it, Mr. Helm?"

"Not quite yet," I said. "Don't be so quick to hand over the baby, Decker. You two are off the hook when Mrs. O'Leary and I are on the plane and it's airborne, not before. Have you got some airline schedules and a map of Mexico?"

Without speaking, Priscilla went over to the dresser, picked up several gaudy folders, and held them out for me to take.

"You know your own business, I suppose," she said when I came over and took them. "But is it wise to announce your intentions quite so loudly, Mr. Helm? I can't guarantee that we're not being overheard. There are too many ways of bugging a hotel room, and I'm sure the glamorous lady for whom you just bought a drink, down there on the beach, knows most of them."

Her voice had a strongly disapproving note. As I say, some people have a thing about fraternizing with the enemy, particularly when the enemy is female and attractive.

"She does at that," I said cheerfully. "Incidentally, her code name is Vadya. I mention it in case you haven't got around to identifying her yet. What name is she using around here?"

"She calls herself Baum. Valerie Baum."

"What, if anything, do you have on her?"

"Not much to date. Now that you've given us the code name, maybe we'll have more."

"Have you spotted any helpers hanging around?"

"No. She seems to be working alone."

"Not according to her," I said. "At least she says she's

expecting reinforcements—a gent named Harsek. About forty, about five ten, about two twenty, substantial but not flabby. Customarily shaves his head and packs a Luger. Have you spotted anybody like that?"

I put the question to Hartford, to keep him in the conversation. He shook his head, as did Priscilla, who asked rather tartly: "Did Mrs. Baum—Vadya tell you all this?"

"She gave me the name. I study the dossiers occasionally, and I've got a good memory. Of course, if Vadya says she's waiting patiently for Harsek to get here, it probably means one of three things: he's here already, or he isn't coming here at all but expects to do the job somewhere else, or she's waiting for some other guy entirely. I mean, Vadya is not a gal whose word I want to rely on very heavily. But we'll keep our eyes open for Harsek just the same." I grimaced. "Haven't you any dope on Vadya at all?"

"Well, we think she was sent to Acapulco to kill a man, a British agent who died there last week under suspicious circumstances." Priscilla glanced towards Annette O'Leary. "But I don't really think we should discuss confidential matters here, if you know what I mean."

I said, "Hell, give your security a rest. We're giving Mrs. O'Leary a tough time; we can at least let her have the fun of watching some real secret agents in action. One more question. That woman you were chatting with at the airport. The blonde with the boyish bob and the football player figure. Where'd you meet her and who is she?"

Priscilla laughed. "Laura Waterman? Oh, she's all

right, just a physical education teacher from California, on vacation. We met in the bar, and it seemed a good idea to cultivate her for company, since Tony was tied up in here when I wasn't, and a woman sitting around alone looks kind of conspicuous. I checked her out first, of course. She's harmless. We have nothing on her, nothing at all."

After a few years in the business, you can generally tell where truth ends and prevarication begins, particularly among the younger members of the profession. The laugh had been wrong and the voice had been wrong: the girl was lying to me. It startled me a little. It opened up, shall we say, vistas of deceit that I hadn't expected to find here.

I said, as if I'd noticed nothing: "Sure. You had nothing on Vadya, either, and you'll seldom meet a more dangerous lady." I went on before Priscilla could think up a suitable retort: "For that reason I'm going to leave the two of you to stand watch in here tonight, while I go out to dinner with her. Maybe I can get a hint of what she and Harsek have in mind. Okay?"

Priscilla said, "I suppose so, but what do you expect to learn from Mrs. Baum?"

"Not much," I admitted, "but she could let something slip, and maybe I can teach her something. Maybe I can convince her that I really mean business. Which brings us back to the question of whether or not she's got this room bugged: the answer is, it doesn't matter. I see that the next plane out of here is the Mexicana jet to Los Angeles tomorrow morning, which makes a reasonable connection with a TWA jet to Albuquerque, New Mexico.

From Albuquerque, I shouldn't have too much trouble reaching Los Alamos; it's only a hundred miles and the roads are good. And I hope Vadya's receiving me loud and clear, because I don't want any misunderstandings. I'm using no tricks and no subterfuges. I'm not going to run, I'm not going to dodge, I'm not going to fight. All I'll do is put a bullet through Mrs. O'Leary at the first sign of trouble, wherever it happens along the way. I hope everybody's got that perfectly straight, including Mrs. O'Leary."

I looked at the red-haired girl as I said it. She licked her lips and didn't speak. I looked back to Priscilla Decker, wanting to ask some further questions: for instance, exactly why she'd been sneaking around watching Vadya and me on the beach, and just what it was that Annette O'Leary had seen out on the water that had got me sent here with such drastic instructions. But the last was very hush-hush information that even Mac hadn't been given, and our Miss Priss was obviously a security nut from way back. On top of that, she didn't like me, and I don't believe in asking questions of people just so they can have the fun of refusing to answer.

I went out and took a taxi to the airport, where I bought a couple of tickets to Los Angeles without any trouble. It took me longer to put a call through to Mexico City, but I finally managed that, too.

5

I took a nap before dinner, not knowing what demands might be made on my wakefulness in the near future. That is, I tried to take a nap, but the telephone aroused me before I had fully dozed off. I picked it up.

"You wanted some information, *amigo*," said the voice of my Mexico City contact. "I have obtained answers to your questions. Do you want them plain or should I fancy them up a bit?"

"Give it to me plain," I said. "If anybody's listening in, to hell with him. Or her. There are too many people being tricky around here without my adding to the number."

"Sí, señor. Your first question concerned the sex of the assigned subject. Washington fails to see the relevance of this, which may be why it was not specified in the original orders. However, since you ask: your subject is female, age twenty-three, and red-haired. You lucky fellow. With respect to this subject, your instructions remain unchanged. Hokay?"

"Hokay," I said. "Carry on."

"Secondly, your descriptions of the agents already on the scene check out perfectly. Is there any valid reason to doubt their identities? If not, just take it you're dealing with the right people and get on with the job. Hokay?"

"Hokay," I said.

"Item number three: a broad-shouldered blonde with a mannish haircut. You asked about her."

"That's right," I said. "I was told locally that she's absolutely harmless. That always makes me suspicious as hell."

"And now, my nosy friend, you are told to stop playing detective and do the assignment you were given in the way it was given you to do. The lady about whom you inquire is none of your business, it says here, friend Eric. I will leave you to guess by whom it was said. That individual states further that I am to do whatever is necessary to make you understand that it is not your job to check up on your associates, or the people they choose to associate with. I am to make it very clear to you that your assignment is only a small part of a larger scheme, the details of which do not concern you, and that's an order! Any comments?"

"Yes, one," I said, and made it.

The man in Mexico City laughed. "Señor, I will forward your brief remark, all four letters of it. *Vaya con Dios*."

It wasn't a conversation calculated to promote a relaxed frame of mind and a peaceful *siesta*, so I put on my damp trunks and took another swim. Bucking the big waves was a good way to use up surplus steam, and I'd generated a certain amount of pressure, being slapped on the wrist like a naughty boy.

Gradually, my temper cooled and my common sense returned. It occurred to me that Mac, although he could be high-handed enough upon occasion, wasn't usually unreasonable and dictatorial towards agents who were merely taking common sense precautions. It could just be, Washington politics being what they were, that he'd deliberately passed along an arrogant message that had been delivered to him, so I'd know there were other forces at work here and govern myself accordingly...

I was in the hotel lobby promptly at seven-thirty. Vadya made me wait only a few minutes before making her appearance.

"Observe the coat and tie as ordered, ma'am," I said when she arrived. "I do believe you have hit upon a new and subtle method of assassination. When I die of heat stroke, it will go down in the books as death from natural causes."

She didn't laugh. "Let's not talk about murder and death tonight, darling, not even in fun. How do I look?"

I guess the question was prompted by the way I was regarding her; I still wasn't quite used to thinking of this smartly slender woman as Vadya. She was wearing a straight, short, sleeveless white dress that touched her only lightly and only in the more significant places. In a way, hinting at untold secrets, it was more provocative than the more obviously revealing white bathing suit had been.

"You look indecent," I said. "Or perhaps the term is

fashionably nude. Have you got anything at all on under that skimpy garment?"

She did laugh at this. "No comment from the lady. I'll let you guess—until the time comes for you to make your determination, shall we say, empirically?"

I grinned. "Jesus, what a complicated way she's got of telling the gentleman she's expecting to be disrobed and ravished later in the evening. Empirically, yet!"

Vadya laughed again, and stopped laughing. "Matt."

"Yes?"

"I am not tricking you. Not tonight."

"Sure." I regarded her soberly for a moment. "And I am not bluffing you, doll. Not tonight. The orders have been given."

"I know." She smiled. "I just heard them played back on the electronic machine."

I grinned. "So you do have the room bugged. Then you know that if anything happens around here while I'm out with you, one person gets a bullet and nobody else gets anything. So let's relax and have fun. What was the name of that restaurant you recommended? The Glass of Milk?"

"Yes, the Copa de Leche. It's downtown; we'll have to take a cab…"

It was a peculiar evening. I mean, this Mexican encounter made the third time we'd run up against each other like this, in the line of duty; and each time before, we'd managed to avoid a fatal showdown, although the last time we'd cut it very close.

Each time before, also, we'd managed to chisel a little

honest pleasure out of all the lies and intrigue. It was an odd relationship we had, perhaps an unhealthy one. It was also a doomed relationship, and we both knew it. Sooner or later our respective superiors would set us on firm collision courses and we'd have to remember that we weren't human beings at all; we were just well-programmed robots representing two great hostile societies.

In the meantime, however, we could at least pretend to be real people. Riding in the cab through Mazatlán we chatted like ordinary tourists, she telling me various things she'd learned about the city and its points of interest. She had the driver show me the view from the top of Icebox Hill, so-called because it held a cave in which, in the days before electric refrigeration, ice from the north was stored. She also had us driven by the docks where a good-sized freighter was being loaded with a certain kind of locally produced seed or grain, the name of which I didn't catch.

The restaurant at which we wound up turned out to be thoroughly modern and, as she'd promised, efficiently air-conditioned, so that I was glad of the jacket I'd been made to wear. The service was excellent and the Martinis were passable, although it's not a drink that Mexican bartenders really understand. The food was very good, even the meat, and they've been known to do some strange things to meat down there.

"Yes, ma'am," I said at last. "I would say this is a thoroughly satisfactory establishment, ma'am, and I take off my hat to your judgment."

She smiled faintly. "And all the time you are wondering

just what is happening back at the hotel, are you not, Matthew? You would very much like to telephone and learn if, perhaps, Harsek has struck already, even though I have assured you that he has not yet arrived on the scene. Why would we have waited if he had? Do you not think we could have got that girl away from those two young agents of yours, Harsek and I? Now that we have you to deal with, it will be more difficult."

I grinned. "I appreciate the flattery. And I'm not really worried about what's happening at the hotel. You've had plenty of chances to deal with the kids already and you haven't done it." I grimaced. "That's what I don't understand."

"What, darling?"

"Just what *is* everybody waiting for? Here you've been sitting on your hands instead of clobbering our two juveniles and walking off with the redhead—and don't tell me you couldn't have done it without Harsek's help. And as for my eager young associates, what the hell have they been marking time for? They could have tried to get out of Mazatlán with the O'Leary, couldn't they, instead of just locking her up in a hotel room and waiting for me. It's almost as if—" I stopped.

"As if what, Matthew?"

"Maybe I'm getting delusions of grandeur, but I've got a funny feeling everybody's been waiting for the dramatic entrance of The Great Helm, in person."

Vadya gave an odd little laugh. "You *are* getting conceited, aren't you, darling?"

"No," I said. "Not really. Because my funny feeling says everybody's been waiting for me to make a patsy of me somehow." There was a space of silence. I knew that I'd got hold of the thin, tail end of a shining truth, and I knew that, now I had it, I might as well let it go, for the moment. Vadya knew she'd made a slip and wouldn't let it happen again. I made a face and said plaintively, "Well, I just wish I knew what the hell is going on around here. What did that red-haired girl see out on the water, anyway?"

Vadya laughed. "If we knew, we wouldn't be so anxious to have her tell us, would we?"

I said, "To hell with that. You know *what* it was; what you want is details, not simple identification. Something apparently landed in the drink out there, something that's got a couple of large nations very worried indeed. Flying saucers, for God's sake! Your people must have pretty strong reasons for climbing out on *that* limb! They're even less fond of getting themselves laughed at than we are."

Vadya smiled faintly. "Are you trying to get me to tell you how much we know? You are wasting your time. And if you're going to be dull and serious, I want to leave."

"You started it, teasing me with what Harsek might be doing, back at the ranch," I said. "Hell, I don't think there is any Harsek. Or if there is, he's doing the Lawrence bit over in Arabia somewhere, camel, burnoose, and all. With his little Luger clutched firmly in his sandy little fist. No dessert?"

"No, thank you. Their desserts are too starchy for my glorious new figure."

"Brandy?"

"No, darling. I am not in the mood to make a drinking night of it. Just take me back to the hotel and make love to me."

I grinned and started to make a smart-alecky response; then I saw that her face was serious, maybe even a little sad, and I cut off the humor, paid the bill, and escorted her outside. We were greeted by rain-wet pavements and a crash of thunder; a tropical storm had sneaked up on us unheard while we were having our air-conditioned meal. I beckoned to a taxi waiting in front of a neighboring hotel, and we made a dash for it as it pulled up.

It had only one functioning windshield wiper, and that on the wrong side to be of any help to the driver, but he seemed accustomed to flying blind, and brought us to the Hotel Playa unscathed. I paid him and hurried after Vadya down the side of the hotel, more or less sheltered from the rain by the balcony serving the second-floor rooms above. She stopped at a door and turned to face me, a little breathless, holding out a key.

"Here we are," she said. "Matt?"

"Yes?"

"Do you remember the motel in Tucson? And that nice lodge up in the Scottish Highlands?"

"I remember," I said.

She hesitated, as if to say more; then she drew a long breath, like a sigh, and said, "Well, you've got the key, darling. What are we waiting for?"

I looked at her sharply. It seemed to me she was

making a little more of opening a door than was absolutely necessary. Her face told me nothing. I unlocked the door and stepped aside to let her pass. I followed her inside and waited as she reached for the switch.

The light came on, and the man in the bathroom doorway fired.

6

It was a silenced pistol, which made it an automatic because, despite what you may have seen on TV, revolvers aren't really amenable to silencing. The necessary clearance between the front of the rotating cylinder and the rear of the fixed barrel lets out too much noisy gas regardless of what magic gizmos you screw on the muzzle. The little plopping sound meant that it was a fairly small-caliber gun, probably a .22. The big blasters can't be quieted so effectively, at least not by any device you'd want to smuggle into somebody's hotel room.

I don't mean I stood there figuring all this out; but it's always useful to know what kind of a weapon you're up against. As I got my reflexes working, I kept in mind that I was dealing with a fast-firing little gun probably holding in the neighborhood of ten shots, a gun with which the other guy would have to hit me dead center, since he didn't have much shocking power at his disposal. Not that any pistol will really knock a man off his feet, but since the ambusher had missed his first shot I did have a bit of a fire-power edge with my heavier .38 special—if I could get it out in time.

I couldn't use my right hand. That angle was blocked by Vadya, probably deliberately. I remembered the sadness I'd seen on her face when she'd suggested coming back here; and her odd hesitation outside. I remembered also that she did owe me a bullet for old times' sake. Apparently this was the payoff. Well, one shot had already been fired and I wasn't dead.

All kinds of fragmentary thoughts like this were flashing through my mind, but I was already going for the gun in my belt left-handed, twisting it free as I dove to the side. The maneuver is fairly awkward, and while I'm a pretty good shot I'm not really an expert gun-juggler. My performance wouldn't have earned any applause from the boys with the big hats and the tied-down holsters who play fast-draw games with electronic timers. The silenced gun had time to spit once more before I could get lined up properly, but I still wasn't hit.

Then the sawed-off .38 in my hand went off with a deafening report. I mean, in a situation like that, if you've had the training and practice, your gun kind of fires itself as it comes on target. I gave it free rein, so to speak: I don't insist on economical one-shot kills. I'm willing to waste a little ammunition to insure that the other guy gets dead and I stay alive. I let the gun keep firing until the target went down.

It took three shots. Suddenly the room was very quiet

again, until lightning flashed and thunder roared outside. I listened intently afterwards, expecting to hear excited voices and hurrying footsteps coming my way, but the hotel was silent. Whatever noises had been heard beyond this room, they'd apparently been attributed to the storm— or to the Mexican kids and their inevitable firecrackers.

I drew a long breath and shifted the revolver from my left hand to my right, which shoots better. Not that the left had done too badly tonight. Belatedly I looked around for Vadya. I found her lying on the floor almost at my feet.

This wasn't on the program, or what I'd thought was the program. It was her room and her ambush, wasn't it? She wasn't supposed to be hurt; I was.

Bewildered, I glanced at the man I'd shot, lying face down across the bathroom threshold. He was wearing a light suit, almost white, but dark blood was crawling out from under his motionless body in large quantities and spreading across the tiled floor. I didn't have to worry about him. They don't make trouble when there's that much blood.

I knelt beside Vadya and lifted her gently. There was some blood here, too; a round stain of it on the white dress over the breast, and a trickle across the face. She'd taken both of the dead man's bullets, and both had been placed squarely in the spots most vulnerable for a small-caliber weapon: the heart and the head. One could have been an accident, not two.

I sighed and lowered her carefully to the floor and stood up. Things were becoming a little clearer, but no more pleasant. I walked grimly over to the body in the bathroom doorway and raised it a bit with my foot, enough so that I could see the face. By this time I wasn't really surprised to learn that it wasn't a man at all.

It was the short-haired blonde lady Priscilla had identified as Laura Waterman, the California gym teacher with the fullback figure. She was wearing one of those idiot pantsuits that have recently come into style, with a man-tailored jacket and sharply creased trousers: a real natty gent's outfit complete to soft silk shirt and flowing tie. Well, if they will dress like men, they can't complain if they get shot for men when things get hectic.

I was glad to see that, as I'd guessed, the gun was a silenced .22 automatic. At least I'd been right about something.

I drew a long breath and went back to Vadya. I didn't lift her this time. I just crouched beside her body briefly and had some thoughts. They weren't very nice thoughts. Obviously she'd sensed that she was being set up for the kill—the touch, as we call it—and most likely she'd thought I knew all about it. Perhaps she'd even credited me with planning it. Yet she'd walked right into the room ahead of me. I would probably never know why. I didn't even want to know why. Perhaps she'd just known that the game was over between us, although that was a bit of sentiment I wouldn't really have expected to influence her to such an extent, flattering though the thought might be.

I got up slowly and went to the phone and asked for room 116. When a girl's voice answered, I said, "Priscilla, get over here right away."

"Mr. Helm? Where—"

"Cut it out," I said. "You know where. On the double. And tell Hartford to lock the door behind you and stay awake."

I hung up and sat on the bed with my thoughts and my gun until she knocked on the door. Then I rose and walked over and yanked it open, letting it swing wide of its own accord while I took a quick step in the other direction. Most room-entering techniques are based on the assumption that the man inside the room will go the same way as the door he's opening for you, and there was an instant, looking for me over there, when Priscilla was off guard.

I said, "You see, you did know where to come." She spun around to face me. I said, "Sweetheart, if that purse swings five degrees more in my direction, or if there's anything in your hand when it comes out of there, this room will be just loaded with corpses. Now bring it out empty like a good girl. That's better."

"Mr. Helm, what in the world…?" Her voice stopped. Her eyes widened. "*Laura!*"

"Hold it!" I snapped as she started forward. "First, the purse. On the bed, if you please. Second, watch your step. We don't want to go tracking a lot of gore around the place, do we?"

She put the purse on the bed without taking her eyes from the motionless form sprawled in the bathroom doorway.

"Laura!" she breathed, and went on without looking in my direction: "You… you *killed* her!"

"That's right. I killed her. But who did I kill?"

That brought her head around sharply. "You know perfectly well—"

"Sure. You told me. A schoolteacher on vacation, a harmless lady tourist from California. A tourist who opened up with a silenced gun when I stepped into this room. What was I supposed to do, take your word for it she was harmless while she was blasting away with her little .22?"

Priscilla licked her lips. "You're being ridiculous! You'll never get away with this, Helm! You're going to pay for it. You've killed a fellow U.S. agent—"

It was what I'd already guessed, and having my guess confirmed didn't really make me happy, but there was no need for her to know that. I just sighed in a relieved sort of way.

"At last. Somebody has finally admitted, now that she's dead, what the dame actually is. Or was."

"You can't stand there and pretend you didn't know—"

I said patiently, "Look, doll, I just saw the woman once outside this room, in the airport with you. Something about her made me curious. I had a hunch she was someone I ought to know more about, so I asked you. You gave me the harmless-tourist runaround. Being a persistent fellow, I reported your story through channels and asked for the real dope. That got me a slap-down from my boss, who obviously got some kind of security door shut in his face when he passed my innocent query along. Apparently he was told to inform me that the lady was none of my goddamn business, and he did. Well, anybody who shoots at me is my business…"

"She wasn't shooting at *you*!"

"Sweetheart," I said, "when I walk into a room and a gun goes off in my face, it's shooting at me. At least I operate on that assumption until I learn different. Unless I'm warned in advance, and I wasn't warned." I looked into the girl's pale face and angry eyes. "Why wasn't I warned, Miss Decker? You presumably took Miss Waterman to the airport to identify me for her. Why were you all so dead set against identifying her for me?"

She didn't answer the question. She just said insistently, "But you must have recognized her, right there across the room with the light on. It was on, wasn't it?"

"Sure it was on." It was like arguing with a stubborn, stupid child, but I kept trying. "But even if I'd recognized her, so what? I'd asked for identification twice and got a negative answer both times. That made her just a stranger with a gun, shooting." I grimaced. "And as a matter of fact, all this is beside the point, because I didn't recognize her in that damn transvestite outfit she had on."

Priscilla's breath caught. "Really, Mr. Helm! That's a perfectly respectable and fashionable costume these days, and you have no right to imply—"

"I wasn't implying anything. I was just saying flatly that the dame was dressed like a man, at a hasty glance, and I had no reason to be considerate of a man of that general description. Nobody'd told me to watch what I shot at. Okay, so it turns out you had a trap set for Vadya, and I suppose you were more or less using me for bait. Fair enough, but why wasn't I warned?"

Priscilla glanced at the still, dead figure in the white dress, lying at her feet. She brought her glance back to my face. When she spoke, her voice had its familiar prim inflection.

"How could we warn you, Mr. Helm? We knew of your past record of association with this woman. We knew that you'd been under orders to kill her, if possible, a year or so ago, and only managed to wound her. For a man of your experience and reputation, that was a very Freudian mistake, Mr. Helm, if it *was* a mistake. And after the fond way I'd seen you greet her down there on the beach—an enemy agent high on the priority list!—how could we warn you and risk having you alert her?"

I'd been in the business too long to blow a fuse just because a sanctimonious kid cast aspersions on my loyalty. I said, "Next time I meet a beautiful enemy agent, I'll remember to knock her teeth down her throat for the benefit of any juvenile U.S. Mata Haris who may be snooping around. Proceed."

Priscilla went on stiffly: "The woman had to die, not only because she was on the list, but because she's been interfering with our work, both here and in Acapulco—it was one of our agents she killed there, not a Britisher as I told you. You're right in thinking you were brought here partly to distract her from the trap we were setting—as bait, if you like. We were hoping that, once you were in Mazatlán, Vadya would concentrate on you and more or less ignore us, as she did. But there was reason to believe that your emotions were involved where this woman was concerned; we simply couldn't gamble on taking you into our confidence."

"Sure," I said sourly. "I congratulate you on your discretion. I'm sure Miss Waterman is very happy that security has been preserved." I went on before Priscilla could speak: "Well, we've got a nasty mess on our hands. Let's figure out what we're going to do about it while there's still time."

I glanced down at the short-barreled revolver I still held. After a moment, I carefully smudged a couple of fingerprints that might have been classifiable, and bent over to lay the gun near Vadya's outflung hand. Then I picked up her purse and got her gun: a little Browning 9mm pocket automatic, shooting the short cartridge also designated as .380, not the huskier 9mm Luger load. I tucked this inside the waistband of my pants and looked at the girl still standing by the bed.

"Do you get the sketch, or do I have to draw it for you?"

"They shot each other, is that it?"

"Very good, Miss Decker," I said. "So now what do you do?"

"Why, I—" She stopped uncertainly.

I said, "First of all, you search her luggage discreetly to make sure she hasn't any spare ammo kicking around. It wouldn't do for her to be found with a .38 Special gun and .380 ammunition; the rounds are not interchangeable.

And then you get your people in Washington on Operation Coverup, real quick. We're not going to fool the Mexican police if they don't want to be fooled, but perhaps, with a little diplomacy, the desire can be created. Check with your superiors. Find out if they can get local cooperation somehow. If not—" I paused, thinking hard. "What about Mrs. O'Leary? Does Los Alamos really want her, or was that just camouflage for your fancy mousetrap?"

"Of course Los Alamos wants her! This was just a... a side issue. We were killing two birds with one stone."

I said, "Well, two birds got killed, all right. Okay, I take the O'Leary north as planned. The plane is supposed to leave at nine-ten tomorrow morning, but it's been known to be quite late. It's supposed to arrive in Los Angeles at eleven-thirty-five, but we'd better allow for the possibility of a two-hour delay, at least. And as long as we're in the air, over Mexican territory, we can be called back. Therefore I'm not really in the clear until I'm on the ground in Los Angeles. You see the problem, I hope."

"I think so. Go on."

"If your people assure us they can count on getting cooperation here, swell. But if not, you've got to keep the hounds off my trail until around one-thirty tomorrow afternoon. How you do it is your business."

She looked at me bleakly. "Thank you very much, Mr. Helm. It sounds like a lovely assignment."

I grinned. "Glad you like it, ma'am," I said. "Okay, I'll give your regards to Mr. Hartford now, and take the subject off his hands." I hesitated. "Are you sure you can handle things around here?"

That stung her youthful pride, as it was supposed to do. "I can handle them," she said stiffly. "Don't worry about me!"

"That'll be the day," I said, and I walked out of there without looking at the bodies on the floor, either of them.

7

As I moved away, I had the feeling I was leaving something important behind in that room, and maybe I was, but it wasn't anything I could ever go back for. I went quickly to number 116 and knocked. The door opened cautiously. Seeing me, Hartford put his gun away and stepped aside to let me in. His tanned, boyish features looked kind of pale and shocked.

"Priss just called," he said. "God, Mr. Helm, it's terrible! Poor Laura! I don't know what to say!"

I said callously, "Well, that's what happens when you try to kill two birds with one stone and don't bother to let the stone know what's expected of it. I guess we've kind of loused up part of the job, although it got done after a fashion. But let's see if we can't handle the rest of it a little better."

"Sure, Mr. Helm."

I looked at Annette O'Leary, watching us silently from the big chair she still occupied. "I'll take over now," I said to Tony. "I'll take her to my room and keep an eye on her until it's time to go. I'll need her tourist permit to get her out of Mexico, and then I'll need proof of her citizenship and a recent vaccination to get her into the U.S."

"Her papers are all in her purse, in the suitcase." He indicated the green bag on the luggage stand.

"That's hers? Swell, I'll take it. Come on, Mrs. O'Leary."

The girl rose reluctantly and put her feet into the white pumps standing by the chair. The high heels made her look taller, but she still wasn't anybody you'd turn to look at, except for the flaming hair. I couldn't help thinking of a woman I'd known who'd managed to look a lot more interesting, even when masquerading as a mousy brunette or faded blonde...

But that was beside the point, now. Picking up the suitcase, I moved towards the door. Tony stirred uneasily.

"But I don't know what you want... I mean, don't you have some instructions for me?"

I stopped to look at him. "Sure," I said. "Go to bed and get a good night's sleep."

"But..." He hesitated. "In the morning, don't you at least want me to cover you on the way to the airport?"

I said, "If I did, I wouldn't tell you about it here: I have it on good authority that this room is wired for sound. But just so everybody's got everything perfectly clear, including Mr. Harsek if he's listening in, I'll say it once more: I'm using no cover and no tricks. I've got nothing up my sleeve. All I've got is a 9mm Browning pistol with six cartridges in the magazine and one in the chamber. If anything happens, or starts to happen, or even looks as if it just might happen, between here and Los Alamos, New Mexico, that pistol goes off. And whatever this lady might have said to anybody just doesn't get said. Let's go, O'Leary."

She moved past me reluctantly. I followed her out into the night. The rain had stopped, but water still dripped from buildings and trees, and thunder rolled in the distance. We proceeded along the walk to my room, which differed from the one we'd left only in that the beds stood out from the wall side by side like beds, instead of masquerading as sofas. I threw the suitcase on the nearest one, and extracted the white purse nesting among the clothes inside. It held a current American passport, an international health certificate with several immunizations including smallpox properly validated, a Mexican tourist card, and a book of travelers' checks, as well as the usual feminine maintenance equipment and supplies.

"If you're through with it," Annette O'Leary said grimly, watching, "if you're *quite* through with my purse, may I have it please?"

I took the essential documents, checked the purse for weapons and found none, and gave it to her. I watched her go to the dresser and do a little repair work in front of the mirror. Normally, I find that there's something kind of sexy about a woman combing her hair, particularly long hair, but tonight I got no kick out of the performance. She was just a skinny kid fixing her hair and to hell with her.

"You're really pretty incredible, dad," she said without looking around. "So you're going to shoot me just like that!" She closed her purse with a snap and brushed hairs off her shoulders. Then she pulled down her jersey and smoothed down her skirt and made a wry face. "God, I look like a tramp who's been sleeping in the woodshed!"

The green jersey looked all right to me—you can't do much to jersey—but now that she was standing up I could see that the brief white skirt was a little mussed and grubby. Well, it's only in the movies that the heroine can endure days of cruel captivity without a few smudges and wrinkles to show for it.

I grinned. "What's the matter, wouldn't they let you change your clothes?"

"Don't be silly. I wasn't about to let them get my clothes off without a fight. They'd have left me sitting there in bra and panties, or nothing but a towel, just to make sure I wouldn't try to escape. There's nothing as helpless as a girl in her undies." She gave me a sideways glance. "I mean, of course, as far as *escaping* is concerned."

I grinned again. She was a pleasant change from Missy Prissy and her sanctimonious expression. "Speaking of helplessness," I said, "why didn't you try doing a little work on Tony while you had the chance? Or did you?"

"That creep? Ugh." Her voice expressed total revulsion. "Besides, I'm not sure he really *likes* girls, if you know what I mean. Come to think of it, I'm not sure *she* really likes boys."

The sharpness of her tone reminded me that she

had good reasons for prejudice, not to say malice. Nevertheless, the possibility she suggested was one that had already occurred to me. After all, the fake lady gym teacher had been a fairly typical specimen. On the other hand, I reminded myself, we sometimes have to put on some fairly unsavory impersonations in the line of duty. Anyway, their sex life wasn't my worry.

Annette O'Leary said, "You haven't got a drink around here, have you, dad?"

"Sure. If you don't mind bourbon."

"It sounds but heavenly-divine. Just between you and me, I'm getting pretty damn tired of all the quaint local concoctions of rum and tequila. Have you tried a Coco Loco yet? They serve it in a coconut, using the milk for a mixer, for God's sake... Thanks."

I watched her gulp the drink I handed her, while I sipped at my own more cautiously. Presently she turned to look at me again with suspicion in her eyes.

"You're a fast man with a glass, dad. And you don't seem to be working very hard on your own. Could it be that you wouldn't mind if I got just a wee bit drunk?"

I said, "Hell, you asked for it. If you don't want it, flush it down the john."

She was watching me closely. "If I did get just a wee bit drunk, what would you do? Would you take advantage of my inebriated condition, and if so, how? I mean, would you seduce me, or just ask me a lot of silly questions?"

I said, "I'll be honest with you, Mrs. O'Leary. At the moment you interest me, biologically, just about as much as that chair over there. For seduction, you'd better come back tomorrow or the next day."

There was curiosity in her look now. "You mean… you mean killing somebody affects you like that? Oh, I heard Tony-boy talking on the phone about what a trigger-happy character you are. But I always thought a man wanted sex after blood, so to speak. Is it because you made a mistake, or because it was a woman you shot?"

I said, "O'Leary, you're a ghoul."

Her greenish eyes were watching me intently, back in the shadow of all that hair. "Oh, I see! It's not *that* woman that bothers you, it's the other one who got killed tonight. The one you went for in a big way, so they said. Mr. Helm, is this your quiet way of mourning the dead?"

I grinned. "You bitch," I said. "You need another drink."

When I came back with it, she was sitting on the end of one of the beds with her shoes off. "How long does the effect generally last, dad?" she asked, taking the glass. "I mean, do you lose your manhood with every dame who dies or goes off and leaves you, and if so, what brings it back and how much later?" She studied me in a speculative, malicious way. "I bet I could bring it back. Tonight. If I really wanted to. And I've never slept with a killer. It might be fun. Cool. At least you don't spend half the day combing your peroxide locks, like the other one. God, I can't stand a man who keeps fussing with his lousy hair."

I laughed. "You know, I'm going to miss you if I have to shoot you. You're quite a girl. Well, let's hope nobody pushes me into a spot where I have to use the gun. Which reminds me—"

I sat down on the other bed and took out Vadya's automatic and checked it over. I don't ever really trust a weapon that's been loaded by somebody else, even by a pro like Vadya. I heard the redhaired girl make a small sound, like a sigh. She finished off her drink abruptly.

"You win, dad," she said softly. "I was trying to needle you, but you topped me. Put the damn thing away, please... Helm?"

"Yes?"

"I'm scared. Do you know that? I'm scared silly. What the hell have I got myself into, anyway? Please put it away."

"Sure, Mrs. O'Leary."

"Don't keep calling me that. It makes me think of the lady whose cow burned up Chicago. Call me Netta, if you've got to call me something."

"Sure, Netta. I'm Matt."

"Hit me again, will you, Matt," she said, holding out her empty glass. "I might as well be good and drunk as the way I am. And if you really have some questions you'd like answered, go ahead and ask."

Bartending again, I said in what I hoped was a casual tone of voice, "Okay, if you insist. Just what the hell did you see out there on the water that's so damned important?"

"Your prune-faced girlfriend has already taken that story down on tape. Why make me repeat myself?"

"Because some gents in Los Alamos have that tape by now, and I don't really expect them to play it for me," I said. "And I'm getting kind of curious about what kind of a yarn you spun for them. Try it on me."

She looked up at me as I returned with her drink. "You don't sound very much as if you were planning to believe me."

Again, it seemed like a situation in which skepticism might be more productive than faith. I said, "Well, I'm not much for ghost stories. Or science fiction, either. But I'm willing to be convinced."

Resentment showed in her small, freckled face. She said sharply, "Well, believe it or not, what I saw was a flying saucer after it had broken down and stopped flying. I saw it right up close, as close as anybody has."

"Don't give me that," I said. "I've read plenty of reports of wild-eyed citizens who've claimed to have been taken right aboard the things. Did you go on board?"

"Well, no," Netta admitted. "God, no! I just scrunched down in my life-jacket and tried to look like a piece of flotsam. Or jetsam. They weren't exactly friendly and hospitable, if you know what I mean."

"No, I don't know, exactly," I said. "What did they do to indicate their hostility?"

"They blasted the boat as they came over. Is that hostile enough for you? I'd gone out with Phil and another couple—"

"Phil?"

"A guy I'd met up north of here, in Guaymas. That's where I stayed first in Mexico: The Posada San Carlos, in Guaymas. Nice place. He was there for the fishing, but it wasn't much good, and he heard it was better down here in Mazatlán, so he decided to drive down. I rode with him. It's a day's drive. He was a pretty nice guy. I don't dig fishing one little bit, but I don't mind sitting in a boat, watching, as long as there's a shady spot so I don't sunburn too badly. He got another couple to share the expenses. I mean, the boat charter or rent or whatever you call it is pretty steep, something like forty dollars a day. I don't remember their names and it doesn't matter. They're dead and so's Phil. If the ray or whatever it was didn't get them, they were killed when the boat blew up."

"Ray?" I said, trying to convey a hint of a sneer. "You mean like in death ray?"

She shrugged. "Don't ask me what it was. I guess maybe they wanted that piece of ocean all to themselves to land in. I was down in the cabin getting a beer; I didn't know what the hell had happened. There wasn't any noise; just a big shadow passing over the boat, and a sudden blast of heat, and flames everywhere. I tried to get back out to where the others were, but the whole cockpit or whatever you call it was on fire. I grabbed a life preserver and scrambled out an opening onto the forward deck. It was burning in spots, too; that's how I hurt my arm. I guess it was the gas tanks that blew up, right after I jumped." She grimaced. "Then there was just one O'Leary in the water, and some floating wreckage, and this damn *plativolo*, sinking."

"*Plativolo*," I said. "That's a new name for it. New to me, anyway. You saw it sink?"

Netta nodded. "Well, I saw the end of it, let's say. They were scrambling around trying to keep it afloat, but they weren't having any luck. And then they blew up, too. Bang, just like that. A great big searing whoosh of flame, like the end of the world. Stuff raining down for minutes, it seemed like. Then I paddled around for a while all alone until somebody came out to investigate the fireworks and picked me up." She shook her head ruefully. "I should have kept my trap shut about what I'd seen, I guess. I should have said the boat just caught fire and exploded. Just call me Public-spirited Patsy for short."

"And that's what all the excitement is about?" I said in a cynical voice. "Hell, I've read fancier Youfoe stories in the papers. Complete with little Martians in metallic play suits." I kept my voice casual. "You haven't said what *they* looked like."

Netta laughed softly. "So I haven't, dad. That'll cost you another drink."

"My God, the girl's got a hollow leg." I fixed her up again, and stood over her. "Okay, give."

She drank from her glass, and looked up, shaking her head solemnly. "No, to hell with you. You've decided I'm just making it up as I go along. Haven't you? Even if I said they were human, you wouldn't believe me."

I grinned at her mockingly. "But they weren't human, were they, Carrots? It wouldn't make as good a story if they were human. They were giant grasshoppers, or little bitty manikins with great big brainy heads and no hair. Come on, O'Leary. Let's hear what you told the tape recorder. Let's hear what that redheaded Irish imagination produced to impress the suckers. I bet it was as good as a TV show: the people from outer space are upon us; the conquest of Earth begins; E-day is here! Is that it?"

She didn't answer at once. She was getting pretty tight; it showed in her careful movements and owl-solemn expression and unladylike, legs-apart posture, sitting there on the bed. When she spoke again, her voice was thick and the words were slurred.

"Damn you!" she blurted. "Damn you, you think you know everything, don't you? Well, I don't give a damn what you think! They *were* human, damn you. They were ordinary human men in ordinary human uniforms, how do you like that? Ordinary U.S. Air Force uniforms! And that overgrown dish they were flying had U.S.A.F. insignia on it. And how do you like *that*, Killer Helm…?"

8

In the morning, I got up stiffly from the chair in which I'd spent the night—what had been left of it after Netta had passed out on the bed. I went into the bathroom and shaved without closing the door.

I've heard of men who have great ideas while shaving, but it's never happened to me, and it didn't now. Even after a wakeful night to work on it, I couldn't decide what to think about what the girl had told me. Of course, it did explain certain things, for instance why I'd been sent here to bring her back or shut her up permanently.

Obviously somebody in Washington, after hearing the taped interview, had panicked at the possibility that she might blab her story around. The idea that the U.S. was operating strange and dangerous flying machines over friendly foreign territory, and blasting friendly foreign boats and citizens with death rays in the interest of total secrecy, was one that the image-conscious gents in the nation's capital would feel must be kept from spreading by any means, no matter how drastic. This could well apply whether the idea was true or false.

But the main questions remained unanswered: was the kid actually telling the truth, or what she thought was the truth, and if so, just what had she really seen?

On the one hand, I knew of no reason for her to lie—which didn't mean that none existed. On the other hand, her story wasn't very plausible, at least not to a patriotic American who loyally endorsed his Air Force's scoffing attitude towards pies in the skies. To such a steadfast citizen, the thought that the U.S.A.F. might have had something up its sleeve all the time it was dismissing various odd celestial phenomena as marsh gas or the planet Venus, would of course be unthinkable.

Unfortunately, many people in the world had always been sadly skeptical about our flyboys' pronouncements concerning UFOs. This included even Americans who, like me, had seen things in the heavens they couldn't explain. And the disturbing fact was that the events the girl had described could easily have taken place pretty much the way she'd described them. You didn't even have to subscribe to her "death ray" to believe the rest of the story.

Say that a secret, experimental U.S. aircraft, crippled and on fire, had descended into the sea, shedding some flaming debris that just happened to land on top of an innocent Mexican fishing vessel. To a girl in the water, dazed and scared, the half-submerged wreckage of the plane—whatever its original appearance—could easily have looked like one of the much-publicized saucers of which she'd doubtless seen photos and sketches galore…

Well, it wasn't my problem. I had troubles of my own. First I had to get a hungover and disheveled young lady in shape to appear in public. She groaned when I first shook her, peeked at me resentfully on the second shake, and sat up groggily on the third, swinging her bare feet to the floor and pushing the tangled hair out of her face.

"Oh, God," she said. "What do you want, dad?"

"Not you," I said. "But you might pull down your skirt a bit just the same. It isn't fair to tease the animals."

She tugged ineffectually at the crumpled garment and looked down at herself with distaste.

"Oh, my God," she said. "You might have undressed me. You didn't have to let me sleep it off in my clothes."

"You've got others in your suitcase," I said. "Use them. But first take a couple of these."

She looked suspiciously at the white pills I held out to her. "What's that?"

"Cyanide," I said. "What else? We always carry cyanide pills in our aspirin bottles. You never know when they may come in handy."

She grinned weakly. "I hope you're not kidding. Right now, cyanide sounds swell." She took the aspirin, swallowed it, and washed it down with water from the glass I handed her. She gave me a funny, almost shy little glance. "Did I… I mean, did we… I mean, what the hell happened last night, anyway?"

"You've still got your panties on," I said. "If that's what you mean."

Her grin was stronger this time. "What a waste of good liquor. Do I get to take a shower?"

"If you don't close the bathroom door. I don't think you can make it out through the little window they've got in there, but I don't intend to give you a chance to try. Leave the door open, and answer at once when I speak to you, and I won't peek around the corners. Okay?"

Half an hour later, she presented herself for inspection, slim and boyish in a natty ensemble—pants and jacket—that reminded me unpleasantly of the costume of the woman I'd shot the night before, except that this suit was constructed of some thin printed material featuring a lot of tiny pink-and-green flowers.

Netta read my expression and said, "No like, dad?"

I shrugged. "I once knew a woman who got shot for wearing an outfit like that. Somebody took her for a man and put three bullets into her. But if that's the way you like to look, it's okay with me."

Netta laughed. "You're a funny, old-fashioned kind of character, aren't you?"

I looked at her for a moment. "I may be old-fashioned, doll," I said, "but I'm not funny. Don't make the mistake of thinking I'm just a great big warmhearted daddyo, just because I left your lily-white body alone and didn't peek while you were in the shower. We're going out there now, to pay the hotel bill, take a taxi to the airport, and board the plane. If it's late, as they tell me it often is, we'll wait for it. There may be some opportunities for you to make a break, O'Leary. At least you may think they're opportunities. But on second thought I think you'll see that I didn't get where I am in my line of work by letting little pipsqueak girls run away from me."

She licked her lips. "You don't have to be insulting, Matt."

"Oh, yes, I do," I said. "Because I have to pound something into the space between your ears, whatever it may contain. I've got to make you understand that there are two people in the world who can get you killed in the next ten hours or so. One is a guy named Harsek. The other is you. If either of those people get out of line, you're dead. Well, you can't do anything about Harsek, but you can certainly do something about you, and I advise you to do it."

"All right," she said. "All right, I get the message. I read you loud and clear. I'll be good. What about… what about this Harsek? What do you think he'll do?"

"I don't know," I said. "I don't even know that the man is around. There's been no sign of him. But he was mentioned, and I have to assume he's waiting somewhere along our route, or that somebody is. As for what he'll do, I'm betting on a rifle with a telescopic sight. If he's got a man good enough to drop me instantly with a long-range brain or neck shot…"

Netta shivered. "Don't!"

I grinned. "What's the matter, would you miss me, Carrots? Anyway, whatever he does, it'll have to be fast and effective, if he wants you alive, and he knows it. So if you find me walking and sitting real close to you, it's not just my lecherous nature. I'm doing my best to avoid presenting a clear target to friend Harsek's rifleman, if any. And for this reason I'm afraid we'll have to pass up breakfast. That balcony dining room is a little too exposed. You'll have to settle for a cup of coffee at the airport." I looked at her. "Ready? Okay, here we go."

I let her carry her own bag so that, using one hand for mine, I'd have one free. We got the financial transactions at the desk completed without incident. A bellboy carried the two bags out to the drive and whistled up a cab. I gave him some pesos for his trouble and got in right behind Netta and settled down beside her. Only then did I take time to notice that it was a bright clear morning after the rain.

"The airport, please," I said to the driver. "*Aeropuerto, por favor.*"

"Si, señor."

The taxi was a big old American car that could once have been a pretty fancy town car or limousine. Like all Mazatlán taxis I'd encountered, it had well-worn upholstery and some missing hardware: for instance, the door handle on my side had got lost somewhere. Then, as we drove away, I realized that all the handles had got lost, for doors and windows both.

I brought out the gun, on which my hand had been resting right along. Netta's eyes widened as she saw the blunt, blue muzzle move into line. There was a whirring sound up front, and I was aware that a glass partition was rising from the back of the driver's seat, separating his compartment from ours.

The back of the driver's head caught my attention. He was wearing a dirty khaki cap, but the nape of his neck was clean shaven, something you don't often see down there where haircuts are scarce and skimpy. It was a thick, powerful neck that would suit a strong, chunky man—say a man named Harsek.

I pressed down the safety catch of the Browning. "Sorry, kid," I said, and I meant it.

Netta licked her lips and didn't speak. As I put pressure on the trigger, I heard a small hissing noise. Out of the corner of my eye, I saw some kind of vapor curling from a hole under the front seat.

The whole business was strictly TV. It was so idiotically corny I couldn't quite make myself believe it was happening. I mean, the stuff couldn't be lethal or it would kill the girl as well as me, and in any case it had to reach my lungs to do its work—and any man who's ever pulled a trigger once and knows the way can certainly hold his breath long enough to do it again. Even tear gas wouldn't save the girl, at contact range.

The whole performance was so ridiculous that I hesitated, wondering if I was overlooking something important. I remembered, suddenly, the odd look I'd seen on Vadya's face when I described my orders, a look, almost, of satisfaction. I remembered some other things…

Harsek, up front—if it was Harsek—hadn't looked around, but the tension of the heavy neck muscles proclaimed that he was waiting for the shot. Of course, I could try shooting him, but under the circumstances the seat between us was undoubtedly bullet-proof; and so was the glass and firing at bullet-proof glass at close range is no fun, unless you like picking glass splinters and reflected bullet fragments out of your anatomy. Anyway, nobody'd ordered me to shoot Harsek. My instructions concerned only the girl.

I grinned at Netta, whose eyelids were already drooping from the effects of the gas.

"Next time, doll," I said.

I put the safety back on and returned the gun to my belt. I drew a long, deliberate breath. I mean, why fight it? The sleepy-stuff didn't smell bad at all...

9

I awoke on a studio couch in a familiar living room and wondered how I'd come to be banished from the bedroom. Perhaps there had been a quarrel I couldn't recall, but it wasn't likely, since I'd never come close to fighting with Carol Lujan in the pleasant summer weeks I'd spent here in Santa Fe, New Mexico, after making my escape from the goddamn ranch.

I tried to make the circumstances come back to me, but all I could dredge up was a weird, strangely detailed nightmare about being mixed up in a totally loused-up operation down in Mexico that had ended with me getting myself stupidly trapped, like a TV-style agent, in a gimmicked, TV-style taxi…

I sat up abruptly on the couch, realizing that it had not been a dream, and that this was not my first awakening since. That had taken place in the shabby old limousine on a dirt road somewhere in the coastal forest—call it jungle if you like—near Mazatlán. I'd been quite alone when I awoke. The cab door had been open, and the fresh air had revived me after a fashion, but I hadn't been capable of much coherent thought. I'd just been uneasily conscious of having heard a loud noise that I was supposed to do something about.

Then the sound had come again, and a big jet airliner had passed low over the trees, obviously circling to land somewhere nearby. I'd glanced at my watch: it read ten-fifteen. If it was the plane, I thought, it was almost two hours late, but that, I'd gathered, was not unusual.

I'd remembered fuzzily that back at the hotel a U.S. agent, feminine gender, was chaperoning two corpses, stalling to give me time to get out of the country. It seemed like a very good plan with which to proceed, since there was clearly nothing left to be done here.

Harsek had taken only the red-haired girl and her belongings. I still had my tickets, personal documents, suitcase, and even my gun—well, Vadya's gun. The taxi key was in the ignition. Getting shakily out of the rear of the car, I'd steadied myself against the door to let a wave of dizziness pass. A small, gleaming object on the ground had caught my eye and I'd picked it up mechanically: a fired cartridge case from a 9mm Luger—the Luger, not the Browning. Apparently Harsek had shot at something with his own gun. If his record was a reliable indication of his marksmanship, he'd probably hit it, but there seemed to be no dead men—or girls—lying around.

I'd dropped the fired case. Why should I clean up after Harsek? I'd crawled behind the cab's steering wheel, started the ancient machinery, and headed in the general direction the plane had taken, descending. I'd found my way to the airport in time to join the line of passengers waiting to turn in their tourist cards to the Mexican immigration officials and take off for Los Angeles.

I couldn't remember much about the flight, but I had a very clear recollection of the call I'd made from the L.A. airport when I was safely on U.S. soil once more. Mac had reacted to my report just about the way you'd expect.

"I seem to recall telling you, Eric," he'd said in his coldest voice, "that there is no room for sentimentality in this work. Or sentimentalists, either."

"She was a cute kid," I said deliberately. "The longest, thickest, reddest hair you ever saw in your life. A cunning little face with adorable freckles. I just couldn't bear to shoot holes in her, sir."

"I see." He was silent a long time, apparently giving careful consideration to my words and the tone in which they'd been spoken. "Very well, Eric. We will have to talk with some people in the morning. Under the circumstances, it cannot be avoided. These joint operations are a nuisance, aren't they? Be prepared to tell all about this enchanting young lady you couldn't bring yourself to harm, and exactly why you couldn't bring yourself to harm her."

"Yes, sir."

"I believe the city of Santa Fe is reasonably convenient both to Los Alamos, where the people in question are staying, and Albuquerque, where I'll have to land since there are no jet connections closer. Am I right?"

"Yes, sir. Forty miles one way and sixty the other."

"Very well, I will arrange the meeting for Santa Fe. But there is already a good deal of unhappiness about this affair. Some shooting took place earlier that didn't go quite as planned, I gather. Under the circumstances it might be better if you were not readily available until tomorrow. You can find a place to stay in the area without putting up at a local hostelry, can you not?"

"Yes, sir."

"I thought you probably could," he said dryly. "Give the lady's address and telephone number to the switchboard girl before you hang up. I will call when we're ready for you. Oh, and Eric…"

"Yes, sir."

"Initiative is a commendable attribute in an agent, but I hope you know what you're doing. Don't let your hospitable friend keep you up too late. You will have to think and talk very clearly in the morning."

There had been no question of my staying up late; I'd been practically walking in my sleep when I knocked on Carol's door. I couldn't remember exactly what story I'd told to explain my shaky condition, and being a bright girl she probably hadn't believed it, but she'd let me in anyway, and I'd got my rest and slept the drug residues out of my system. At least my brain seemed to be working clearly once more, if not too happily. I wasn't looking forward to the coming inquisition.

I yawned, sitting there, and looked around. The room

had the usual disheveled look of a living room temporarily converted for slumber. Various items of furniture had had to be shoved aside to let the bed unfold, and it wasn't a very big room to start with.

The clutter was enhanced, if that's the proper word, by a scarred leather camera case of professional dimensions— not one of your jazzy little over-the-shoulder gadget bags—accompanied by a heavy, business-like tripod and a big, beatup box containing, I knew, an assortment of portable lighting units and stands. This was all stacked in a corner ready to go.

The room itself was pleasant in the old-fashioned southwestern way, with the ceiling supported by the bare round beams known as *vigas*, and the windowsills nice and deep due to the thick-walled adobe construction. There was a corner fireplace, the small round kind in which the logs are supposed to burn propped on end, Indian-fashion, which works fine if you can get the same pitchy piñon wood the Indians used, but not otherwise.

The walls were white and covered with carefully arranged groups of photographs, some straight grownup fashion shots, but mostly pictures of child models looking happy and clean and starched and lovable in their pretty clothes. Some framed magazine covers gave color to the arrangements. The pix were technically pretty good, but just a little too sweet for my taste. After all, I'd had some kids once—they're growing up elsewhere with a substitute papa—and they'd never looked like that, even to my prejudiced eyes, except perhaps for a moment or two before church on Sunday morning.

"Well, it's about time you woke up," Carol Lujan said, appearing in the doorway with a tray. "I hope you still take your coffee black and your eggs over lightly, after all your mysterious travels." She came forward. "Just one word of warning: if we should ever get married, don't expect breakfast in bed for the rest of your life. The service is only for hungover gentleman friends who drop in to sleep it off. What's the matter, doesn't your fancy government relations job pay hotel expenses?"

So apparently I'd told her I'd been on a binge, perhaps in the line of duty, say an official reception or cocktail party. Government public relations was the cover story I'd been using since we met earlier in the summer. I mean, it's not considered proper to go around telling people, even nice girls you sleep with, that you're a secret agent.

"Who said anything about matrimony?" I asked, grinning.

"Not you, that's for sure," she said dryly. "Careful now, don't spill it."

She put the tray on my lap and straightened up, a moderately tall, blonde girl with the healthy, well-scrubbed look that's always in style in my fashion book, no matter what kind of bloodless human skeletons may be cavorting on the cover of Vogue this season. She was wearing a brown-checked pleated skirt and a brown pullover sweater with the sleeves shoved casually above the elbows. There were yellow developer stains on her fingers, and there was a wedding ring on her left hand, but the marriage it represented had terminated, I knew, even before my own.

Her maiden name had been Carol Fairweather, and she'd once been married to a pretty good magazine photographer named Ted Lujan—pronounced Ted Loohahn—at a time when I'd had a wife and darkroom of my own. We'd seen as much of each other, back in those days, as two congenial married couples will, living in the same town with the husbands in more or less the same line of work.

Now Ted was dead—a jeep had rolled on him in some backward corner of the world—and my wife, having learned a little too much about my official activities with gun and knife before I settled down to be a private citizen with camera and typewriter, had decided I wasn't the kind of guy she wanted to be married to after all.

This had all taken place several years ago, and I'd managed to avoid Santa Fe ever since, until this summer. Meeting Carol again, in the local bank, had been an odd and not entirely comfortable experience. When you bury the past, you don't really want it to come crawling back up out of the grave.

However, she'd seemed glad to see me, which was flattering, and she was a good-looking girl, and I was alone in town. The least I could do was take her to dinner for old times' sake—and we were unattached adults of opposite sex, and you know how it goes after a pleasant evening of drinks and reminiscences. Now, in a few short weeks, we'd come to know each other well enough that I could even sleep on her studio couch when tired, without feeling obliged to pretend that I really yearned to break down the bedroom door, which wasn't locked anyway.

"What's the matter, Matt? Have I got a smudge on my nose, or something?"

I guess I was looking up at her a little too intently. She was a very attractive girl. They had been pleasant weeks, but they were over. They'd been over a couple of days ago, when I'd got the summons to head south. I wouldn't have come back here at all if it hadn't been for Mac's instructions.

"Your nose is fine," I said. "Did anybody call while I was asleep?"

"No, there have been no phone calls this morning. I guess I'll have another cup of that coffee myself. Just a minute; I'll be right back."

Watching her go out of the room, I had the guilty feeling you get about a girl to whom you've been disloyal, although technically speaking I hadn't managed any real disloyalty, since the lady I'd had in mind for it had got shot before anything could happen between us. Still, I hadn't been thinking very hard about Carol Lujan down in Mexico. The only time I'd used her name, it had been to make another woman jealous. And the lies I had to keep telling her about my occupation were getting a little threadbare and unconvincing. It was really time to go before somebody got hurt.

I buttered my toast while waiting for her to return, and idly read the title of a book on the table: *The UFO Conundrum*. Frowning, I looked at the magazine lying nearby. The cover featured an article entitled: *Flying Saucers: Hoax or Hallucination?* Beneath the magazine was another displaying the catchy line: *I Met the UFOnauts Face to Face!* I tossed the stuff back on the table as Carol came into the room and sat down in a chair facing me.

"Are you expecting a call, Matt?" she asked, stirring her coffee.

"There's a meeting I've got to attend," I said. "They're supposed to phone and tell me where." I glanced at the photographic equipment piled in the corner, and went on casually: "Looks like you're about to take off on a job."

'Yes," she said. "It's a good thing you came when you did. I have to head for Mexico tomorrow, as soon as I can locate a 500mm lens I need."

"Mexico?" I kept my voice even. "What's in Mexico these days in the way of kids or fashions? And what's the camera gag that requires an outsize telephoto lens?"

"I don't *always* shoot just kids or fashions, darling. I get general assignments every once in a while." She hesitated. "I don't know if I'm supposed to talk about it. It's kind of confidential…"

I glanced again at the photographic gear, and at the literature on the cocktail table. I sighed and said grimly, "Don't tell me. Let me guess. Some crackpot magazine editor is sending you to Mexico with a great big long lens to get a close-up portrait of a flying saucer."

"Why, yes," she said, surprised. "Yes, how did you know?"

Across the room, the telephone began to ring.

10

There were four men in the outer sitting room of the hotel suite when I entered, and there were four chairs arranged more or less in a semicircle around a low table. I had a pretty good idea who'd been elected to occupy the sofa upon which the chairs kind of focused.

Mac himself had opened the door for me. He closed it behind me. "This is the man we call Eric," he said. "Sit down over there on the sofa, Eric. Would you care for a cup of coffee?"

I could have used another one, but there are circumstances under which it is not diplomatically correct to eat, smoke, chew gum, or take a drink, even coffee.

"No, thank you, sir," I said.

I went over to the indicated piece of furniture, but I did not sit down. I mean, respect is cheap and looks good, why not utilize it? I waited respectfully, therefore, while Mac seated himself. Then he made a gracious little gesture, and I sat down. I thought his left eyelid half-closed in a kind of wink, as he played up to my phony show of deference, but I could have been mistaken. He wasn't really a winking man.

He looked about the same as the last time I'd seen him, which was about the same as the first time I'd seen him, more years ago than I cared to think about. A lean, gray-haired man with black eyebrows, he was wearing a neat dark-gray suit that might have been designed for a banker, but he was no banker. He was one of the half-dozen deadliest men in the world, and to one in the know, like me, it showed plainly.

The tweedy, affable-looking man next to Mac wasn't deadly. He was only dangerous if you were vulnerable to conniving and intrigue, and if you were stupid enough to turn your back on him. He had a handsome red face, a shock of picturesque white hair, and piercing blue eyes, and he was the coming boy in undercover politics, a character named Herbert Leonard who'd decided that our government's vast civilian intelligence establishment would provide a fertile field for his organizational talents.

He'd already managed to promote himself a new, streamlined agency that would deal with all problems of security and espionage more efficiently—so he claimed—than all us old-fashioned, stick-in-the-mud outfits could possibly do. Obviously he hoped to swallow up or supersede us all in the long run. It was said of him that he envisioned himself as the J. Edgar Hoover of the international cloak-and-dagger set; there were even those who felt that he wasn't totally blind to the fact that

Hoover himself couldn't live forever.

I'd never met him before, but I'd been shown the pictures and told the rumors. I had an uneasy hunch, finding him here, that the U.S. people I'd encountered in Mazatlán would turn out to be his. And if I'd tangled with some of Leonard's protégés, I was in even more trouble than I'd thought.

Next was a man I didn't know, but I bet myself I could place him with reasonable accuracy. He was crowding fifty, but when they get involved with airplanes young— particularly military airplanes—they seem to develop a characteristic Rover-boy look that lasts them the rest of their lives. Some day I'm going to find out what it is about the upper atmosphere that imparts that durable boyish appearance to those who love it. Personally, I age fast whenever I'm off the ground.

Anyway, I was willing to wager a small sum that I was in the presence of a military flyboy with a reasonable amount of rank. He was in civilian clothes—sharp gray flannels—but the eagles or stars show on a man even when the uniform gets left behind.

Next to him was a short, dark, compact gentleman with a thin black moustache. He was obviously foreign, presumably Mexican, in a dark business suit, immaculate white shirt, and silk tie—they don't go in for casual clothes much during business hours. His presence gave an international flavor to the gathering that I found somewhat reassuring. Apparently the purpose wasn't only to give one U.S. agent hell, although that might be first on the agenda.

The white-haired Leonard was the first to speak. "So this is the man called Eric!" he said quickly. "If you don't mind, General, before we start, there are a couple of questions I'd like to put—"

"But I do mind." For all his youthful look, the flyboy could put a snap into his voice. "I have a good idea what questions you want to ask, Herb, and we've already been through all that. You're out of line. I'm not a damn bit interested in your intramural squabbles, for one thing, and for another you haven't got a leg to stand on. I'd never fault one of my pilots, in a combat situation, for returning the fire of an unidentified aircraft when there had been no warning whatever of friendly traffic in the area. As I understand it, this man did everything possible to establish identification, and it was refused. So your agent got shot because somebody got too secretive, and we're sorry about that, but it's got nothing to do with our business here."

Leonard said angrily, "General, I want to point out that I had three good operatives in Mazatlán. One was killed by this man. One was critically wounded trying to rescue him. And the third is presently involved with the Mexican authorities—no offense, Señor Solana—because of her efforts in his behalf. All this for an agent who, when the chips were down, failed to go through with the job he'd been sent to do."

Well, I now at least had a notion what had happened to the bullet from the Luger cartridge case I'd seen. Mac's lips had tightened disapprovingly as Leonard spoke.

He doesn't mind administrative infighting—he's been through years of that—but he can't stand a man who uses "presently" to mean "at present," any more than he can abide anybody who uses "contact" to mean "make contact with." We're all very careful to leave such gobbledeygook usages out of our report. But this was no grammar class, and what he said was:

"Eric, did you request cover from one of Mr. Leonard's agents?"

"No, sir. I told him to get a good night's sleep and lay off. He must have decided to follow me on his own."

Leonard leaned forward triumphantly. "And why *didn't* you ask Hartford to help you? To make doubly sure of carrying out your assignment?"

I said politely, "If I had the situation figured right, sir, I wouldn't need him. And if I was wrong, I figured he couldn't help me much, anyway."

Leonard took the bait. "Why not?"

"Well, sir," I said, making a show of hesitating, "well, sir, Harsek's grade A material, if you know what I mean. He eats little boys like that alive. There was no sense in just setting the kid up for a target." I shrugged. "Apparently he went and set himself up, and got himself shot as could have been predicted."

Leonard's red face was a shade or two darker than it had been. "His interference probably saved your life, Mister! Of course you wouldn't know that, being unconscious at the time."

"Yes, sir," I said. "And if that's true, I'm duly grateful,

but I wasn't aware that saving my life was one of the objectives of this mission. He apparently didn't manage to rescue the girl, which would have been more to the point."

The flyboy leaned forward, interrupting Leonard's retort. "Never mind all that, Herb," he snapped. "I told you to lay off. As for you, son, you've mentioned the objectives of your mission. Maybe you'd better tell us what they were, as you saw them."

It's been a long time since I've been called "son" by anybody, and he'd have had to be kind of precocious to make it as my daddy, but in the armed forces they tend to figure the generations more by rank than by age.

I hesitated. "If it's not classified information, I'd like to know to whom I am speaking, sir."

He looked a little taken aback; then he grinned. "Why, certainly. I believe you know the two gentlemen on my right. I am Brigadier General Bill Bannister, U.S.A.F.— Bannister like in stairs. I'm kind of in charge of this whole crazy operation. And this is Señor Ramón Solana-Ruiz of the Mexican… Well, let's just say that he represents his government here. Very unofficially, of course."

"Thank you, sir," I said. "As for the objectives of the mission as I saw them, they were twofold: to bring a certain young lady to Los Alamos if possible and to kill her if not; also to do this without embarrassing the Mexican authorities if it could be done."

Bannister nodded. "Well, at present the Mexican authorities are embarrassed. And the young lady is neither in Los Alamos nor heaven. Is that correct?"

"I don't know, sir." When he frowned, I explained: "I have no firsthand information about what's taking place in Mazatlán official circles. And I don't know what may have happened to Mrs. O'Leary since I last saw her."

"But you will admit that you were at least partly responsible for some rather embarrassing corpses left behind at your hotel, and that you did not, yourself, carry out the instructions you'd been given concerning the lady."

"That is correct, sir."

Leonard leaned forward aggressively. "The fact is, you spent the night with the girl and she got to you, isn't that it?"

I said, "We certainly spent the night in the same room. It would have been difficult for me to guard her otherwise. As to whether she got to me, or I got to her, I fail to see the relevance of this." I looked towards the general. "It's a principle of the profession, General, that what happens in bed has nothing to do with what happens anywhere else."

He looked amused. "And did anything happen in bed, son?"

"No, sir. But it's a difficult thing to prove, so I won't try."

Leonard said sharply, "In any case, you failed to do your assigned job, didn't you?"

Bannister frowned at the interruption, but said to me: "That's about the size of it, isn't it?"

"Yes, sir."

"Do you have an excuse, or an explanation?"

I said, "I have a reason, sir."

Bannister said, a little irritably, "You don't have to be so goddamn humble, son. I know damn well what you're thinking. You're a tough character—a professional killer, to put it bluntly—and you're thinking that if we lean on you too hard, hard enough to make you mad, you can take the lot of us, just like a fox cleaning out a chicken coop. Am I right?"

He was sharper than I'd given him credit for. I risked a grin and a little impudence. "Yes, sir. And I'd take you first, sir."

"Why? I haven't been giving you as hard a time as some in this room."

I said, "I'd take you first, sir, because I wouldn't want you loose while I took care of the rest."

At this, he grinned back at me. "Flattery will get you nowhere, tough boy. And just go easy on those greasy 'sirs', will you? I get enough of that crap in the service." He cleared his throat. "And now tell us your reason for disobeying orders. You walked into a trap, okay. It happens. Your instructions covered that possibility. If you couldn't get her up here you were to shoot to kill. Why didn't you?"

I said, "Because I discovered that was exactly what they wanted me to do."

11

I won't say it brought down the whole house. Mac didn't look tremendously surprised, and Solana-Ruiz raised his eyebrows slightly, but allowed himself no other reaction. For all I knew, the Mexican had a language problem and wasn't following the discussion in every detail.

But the flyboy general looked startled and interested, as if the idea I'd presented was totally new to him, and rather intriguing. And Leonard's expression showed scornful disbelief, and indignation at my nerve in presenting such an outlandish excuse for my misbehavior, which was about as good a response as I could expect from him.

He demanded, "Do you really expect us to believe—"

Bannister said irritably, "Oh, shut up, Herb! Save the rhetorical questions. Obviously he expects us to believe it or he wouldn't have said it." He looked at me. "Are you sure, son? Positive?"

I said, "Positive, no. But I was sure enough to refrain from pulling the trigger in spite of orders. It looked as if somebody had misjudged the situation completely—"

"The idea is ridiculous!" Leonard snapped. "If Harsek had wanted Mrs. O'Leary dead, he had plenty of time to shoot her himself."

"I don't think that's quite the point," Bannister said slowly. "I think friend Eric, here, has another thought in mind."

"Yes, sir. I don't think Harsek just wanted her dead. I think he wanted her dead at my hands—at the hands of an American agent."

Bannister frowned. "Let's go back a bit, son. You say you 'discovered' this. How?"

"I discovered it when the bullet-proof glass slid up between me and Harsek, and gas started hissing into the rear compartment of the taxi, quite audibly. That was the tipoff. A corny movie routine like that couldn't possibly mean what it was supposed to mean. I don't say the sealed-taxi gag hasn't ever been used in real life, but it's certainly never been used when it was important to immobilize the guy instantly, because there just isn't any such gas as far as I know, and even if there is, they weren't using it. It followed that they didn't want me instantly unconscious. They wanted to give me just a little time before I passed out—time enough to do what they knew I had orders to do. There could be no other reason for them to telegraph their Sunday punch like that."

Leonard said, "You're just rationalizing after the fact! Probably they took a chance on using a rather slow and clumsy technique because they knew you had amorous reasons for not harming the young lady. At least they figured you'd hesitate—"

"On the contrary," I said, "they had no reason to think I'd hesitate at all, that's just the point. All their evidence pointed the other way. I'd warned them repeatedly about what I intended to do if they interfered. And I was the trigger-happy gent who'd just burned down a fellow-agent by mistake because I was so goddamn eager to kill. They had no reason to think I'd wait an instant, given the slightest excuse for pulling the trigger. So they gave it to me." I looked at Bannister. "I'd been under the impression that this girl was valuable to them; that they had to have her alive and talking. When I discovered that was wrong… Well, it seemed best to keep the bullets in the gun until I learned the real score."

The general drew a long breath. "As a matter of fact, son, the orders you received were a little more drastic than necessary or even desirable. Somebody in Washington flipped when he heard the girl's tape, and decided to initiate emergency action without consulting anybody else, including me. So we're not too unhappy about your results, or lack of them. Which of course doesn't excuse you in the slightest."

"No, sir."

"Orders are supposed to be obeyed," he said firmly. Then he grinned a little. "On the other hand, a little common sense isn't a bad thing, particularly in situations involving life and death. Are you aware of what this girl saw, or says she saw, out there in the Gulf of California?"

"Yes, sir."

Leonard demanded, "How did you learn that? It's supposed to be very highly classified."

I said wearily, "As you keep pointing out, Mr. Leonard, I spent the night with the kid. I had a bottle of bourbon and she was thirsty. After a while she started talking."

"You got her tight and pumped her, in other words."

I shrugged. "Nothing in my orders said I couldn't give a girl a drink."

Bannister said, "You're kind of an independent operator, aren't you, Eric? I don't know as I'd want you under my command."

"No, sir," I said, with a glance towards Mac. "Discipline means different things to different commanders, sir. And in our business we can't always get on the radio and check with the home field. Anyway, nobody was telling me anything on this deal, so I figured I'd better find out a few things for myself."

"Well, we'll have you study the taped interview and see if the young lady changed any of her testimony under the influence of your whiskey. But having heard her story, what do you think of it?"

I looked at him for a moment, and let my eyes kind of swing towards Solana, and back. "Do you want me to be honest or diplomatic, sir?"

"We are keeping no secrets from our friends below the border, son. We have no secrets to keep, in this connection."

"Sure," I said. "Well, General, I figure there are three possibilities. One, the girl is lying through her teeth for reasons yet to be determined. Two, she saw a real mystery aircraft with forged markings crewed by men in fake uniforms. Three, she saw exactly what she says she saw, and it's you who are a liar, sir; you're trying to cover up something very hush that went wrong. No disrespect intended, of course."

"Of course." Bannister grimaced, and looked at Mac. "Your people lay it right on the line, don't they?"

"They are supposed to, when asked. You asked."

Bannister turned towards Solana. "You heard, Ramón. Has this man covered the various possibilities considered by your government to explain this sighting and the others?"

"Sí, General. He has expressed it very well. And you will forgive my saying that the last possibility is one that is being considered very seriously. Your official attitude towards these strange aerial manifestations has always suggested that you might have an ulterior motive for wanting them disregarded. I seem to recall UFO sightings officially explained as the planet Venus when that planet was not visible; and radar contacts explained as false readings due to temperature inversions when weather conditions precluded any such phenomena. We have studied the record carefully, General, and always the question arises: why would the U.S. Air Force go to such lengths to ridicule all UFO reports—if it has nothing of its own in the sky that it would like to hide?"

Obviously, Señor Ramón Solana-Ruiz had no language problem whatever. General Bannister winced.

"You're picking at a sensitive nerve, Ramón. I've inherited a loused-up mess. Now we've got the research boys up in Colorado trying to set things straight from the scientific end, while I'm supposed to keep the lid from blowing off in a military and diplomatic way." He turned to me. "You, son. Do you believe in these goddamn saucers? I mean, real ones, not phonies with U.S.A.F. insignia on them?"

"Yes, sir," I said.

"You've seen one?"

"Yes, sir."

"Describe it." When I had, he said, "Oh, the green fireballs. Well, we've got explanations for those, I think."

"Yes, sir," I said. "It used to be marsh gas and now it's electronic plasma or something."

"Are you needling me, son?"

"Yes, sir," I said. "In a helpful way, sir, to emphasize what Señor Solana just said: nobody believes your explanations now. You're in the position of the boy who cried wolf, except that your people have for years been yelling at the top of their lungs that there's no such animal as a wolf. And now folks who don't like us are apparently getting smart and trying to cash in on the general lack of confidence in your pronouncements."

"You think that's what this Harsek was trying to do down in Mazatlán?"

"It seems very likely, sir. He had a choice. Let's assume for the moment that the O'Leary kid actually saw a flying machine of some kind land out there in the drink. Skip the question of whether she lied about the uniforms and markings; just say she did see something and, truthfully or otherwise, attributed it to the U.S.A. Getting wind of this, Harsek's superiors would presumably be interested in two things: finding out as much as possible about the mystery machine itself, and making a propaganda profit from the girl's story. And if it came to a choice, the propaganda she could furnish would be more important to them than the information."

Leonard demanded, "Why? I should think they'd want to know everything they could find out…"

"Sure, but just how much technical information can you expect to get out of a scared girl who saw a strange aeronautical gadget for only a minute or two while she was up to her neck in salt water? How much real information about the thing have you got on your tape? Not much, I'll bet. Anyway, it seems obvious that Harsek got instructions to build up the propaganda angle and let the information go, and that's just what he tried to do."

Leonard looked unconvinced. "By getting the girl shot?"

"By getting her shot by a U.S. agent," I said. "Look, in itself, her story wasn't much. I mean, even if she talked publicly, who's going to take much stock in some weirdie a hysterical kid thinks she saw after jumping out of a burning boat that blew up practically on top of her? But if it gets around that the U.S. is taking her crazy yarn seriously enough to send a team of agents to silence her; if she's actually killed and the American government assassin, me, is caught red-handed; then her wild story will begin to carry conviction, won't it? And the communists will have a propaganda coup that'll lose us a lot of friends in Señor Solana's country, where we haven't got many to spare right now, the way I hear it. Am I right, Señor?"

The Mexican said judiciously, "Certainly the rumor that all these strange sightings are due to secret American aircraft over Mexican territory is not doing the relations between our countries any good, señor. And an incident such as you describe, involving deliberate murder, would certainly have precipitated a great deal of angry talk about Yankee imperialism, perhaps even diplomatic action."

I looked at General Bannister. "I gather from Señor Solana's remarks and yours that the dingus that went down off Mazatlán isn't the only one that's been seen."

Bannister smiled a bit thinly. "Gather what you like, son, just don't ask questions." He grimaced. "Well, is there anything else you'd like to contribute to the discussion before we boot you the hell out of here and talk about things you're not supposed to know about?"

"I can't think of anything, sir."

"What about the O'Leary girl? You met her and talked with her. Do you feel she's lying or telling the truth—what she thinks is the truth?"

"I don't know, sir," I said. "She's a bright kid. She could be a very bright kid putting on a great act. Hell, she could be a skillful communist agent planted in Mazatlán specifically to spread false and slanderous rumors about the U.S.A."

"But you don't think she is?"

I shrugged. "I didn't feel I was dealing with an experienced pro, no, sir. I'd rate her at most as a talented amateur. And I wouldn't be a bit surprised if she turned out to be just a redheaded kid who went fishing at the wrong time."

Bannister glanced at Leonard. "I suppose she's being checked."

"Yes, sir. I have a preliminary report right here. There are some rather interesting things: for instance, both the girl and her deceased husband seem to have been members of a peace group while studying at the University of—"

"Half the kids in college these days seem to have joined those movements," Bannister said impatiently. "Anyway, the man was killed in Vietnam, wasn't he? Apparently his scruples weren't strong enough to keep him out of combat. Well, keep checking and let me know what turns up. Eric."

"Yes, sir."

"Mr. Leonard will give you a transcript of the taped interview. I want you to sit down somewhere and read it carefully. See if it agrees with the story you were told. Make note of any discrepancies. Keep yourself handy. We'll have new instructions for you shortly… and, Eric."

"Yes, sir."

"Obviously you did quite right not to shoot. That gets you off the hook. You can get away with a lot of things as long as you're right." He grinned briefly. "But the independent way you operate, you'd damn well better not be wrong, son, ever. Remember that."

"Yes, sir."

I got a manila folder from Leonard. Mac gave me a key and I went down the hall to his room to do my homework and wait for my orders. I had a hunch they'd be dillies. They were.

12

The following morning was clear and bright and, at that altitude—over a mile high—already crisp with autumn. The four-lane highway leading south from Santa Fe looked fresh and clean, as if it had just been laid down and nobody'd had a chance to mess it up with grease and rubber yet. In the distance, the ten-thousand-foot mountains near Albuquerque were sharply defined against the blue sky.

Carol Lujan's car was a big white Chevrolet station wagon with thick red wall-to-wall carpeting and shiny red leather upholstery—well, vinyl. It had all the power in the world and all the optional equipment that could be hung on it including air-conditioning, which, I reflected, might come in handy when we got farther south and lower down. After all, I hadn't really frozen in Mazatlán.

Surprisingly, in spite of all the automatic and power-assisted gadgetry that tends to bug an old stick-shift man like me, I found the big wagon not too hard to handle. At least it went down the highway quite straight at seventy, instead of wagging its tail unnervingly as so many of them do.

Carol, sitting beside me, reached out suddenly and patted my hand, resting on the steering wheel. "I'm awfully glad you're coming with me, Matt," she said. "I really hate driving, and particularly driving alone."

I let a meaningless grin answer for me, and avoided looking at her. As I've already indicated, the orders cooked up for me had turned out to be real cute. It seemed that Mac hadn't had me spend the night at Carol Lujan's place just to keep me out of sight. Because of my association with her this summer, he'd been having her investigated in routine fashion—our private lives don't stay private long in this business—and he'd been quite interested to learn that she was being sent to Mexico on a UFO assignment. It had seemed to him a coincidence we might well take advantage of—if it was a coincidence. And if it wasn't, so much the better.

"But I've known her a hell of a long time," I'd protested when he'd told me his suspicions.

"Not continuously," he pointed out. "Unless you've been concealing things from this agency, you haven't known her at all for several years. You do not know what connections she may have formed since you ceased your own photographic, journalistic, and marital endeavors and left Santa Fe to come back to work for us. Do you? Are you even quite certain that your happy reunion with the lady was entirely accidental?"

I winced. "That was weeks before I was assigned to this saucer mess, sir," I objected. "If anybody put her onto me with this in mind, they must have been clairvoyant."

"Not necessarily," Mac said. "Has it never happened that an attractive woman has been persuaded, one way or another, to resume a known friendship with a known agent—unfortunately you are becoming pretty well-known in certain circles, Eric—with the expectation that she will prove useful if she should later be given a mission of importance?" Mac shrugged. "In any case, it's a starting point. You will arrange to travel to Mexico with Mrs. Lujan. But in view of the coincidences in which she figures—her making contact with you this summer; her requesting a UFO assignment now—we must leave a large question mark opposite the lady's name." His eyes were cold. "I want you to keep that firmly in mind, Eric."

"Yes, sir."

"Whether justifiably or not, this business is highly classified. Under normal circumstances, I would have no objection to your confiding in the lady if it seemed advisable, but things are not normal in Washington these days. Mrs. Lujan may be guilty or she may be innocent, but one thing is certain: she has no official clearance. And with Mr. Leonard looking for a soft spot in which to insert his well-known dagger, you cannot afford to indulge in any breaches of security, nor can I afford to have you. The very existence of this agency may be at stake. I hope you understand."

"Yes, sir."

"You will lie to her assiduously even in the most tender moments. You will tell her nothing whatever about this agency or its work, and that includes your own duties and responsibilities. You will maintain your cover story—whatever you've been telling her—with a perfectly straight face even if circumstances conspire to render it totally ridiculous."

"Yes, sir," I said.

"Very well. Did you find any discrepancies in the O'Leary statement?"

"No, the kid is either telling the truth or she's memorized her lies well."

"It's too bad you lost her, but under the circumstances your action, or lack of it, was probably justified. At least General Bannister seems to think so. He has asked for you to remain on the case in spite of Leonard's objections. Of course, Leonard's people will be working on it, too, but Mrs. Lujan may give us a slight edge. At least she will give you a reasonably convincing cover. Do you know what her plans are?"

"No, except that she's shopping around for an outsize telephoto lens to snap a saucer's picture with. How she's planning to persuade it to pose for her, I have no idea. I don't think she's ever used one of those long-range optical monstrosities before; I don't think she knows how tricky they are to handle."

Mac said, "Well, I'm sure you can assist her with the technical details, Eric. You used to be a reasonably competent photographer yourself, as I recall. However, you are not being sent into Mexico just to help the lady take pictures."

"No, sir."

"We want the location from which these objects are operating, and we want it as soon as possible. The recent increase in their activity indicates that their efforts will probably reach a dramatic climax shortly, if we are not able to forestall it. You will therefore proceed into Mexico with Mrs. Lujan and persuade her to commence her photographic operations at the scene of the next incident that occurs. We have established that these saucers are quite sensitive about invasions of their privacy. Things seem to happen to people who see them and talk about it—Mrs. O'Leary's disappearance is by no means unique. It follows that even if your attractive photographic friend is not now involved, with a little luck, if she uses her cameras diligently, she soon may be. And of course you will be handy to take advantage of her involvement when it occurs, Eric."

In other words, we were going to use Carol Lujan for bait. It wasn't the best possible foundation upon which to construct a light-hearted alliance with a member of the opposite sex, ostensibly for purposes of travel and photography, and I couldn't help a certain guilty awkwardness now, which I was fairly sure hadn't gone unnoticed by my blonde companion.

"This is quite a heap you've got here," I said casually, to be saying something as we drove. "The photography business must be paying off these days."

Carol laughed. "Well, I'm not quite starving, let's say. Remember when you first taught me how to use Ted's cameras after... after he was killed? And then I went off to work in New York, on your recommendation, and when I came back you were gone, and Beth was packing for Reno, and it was all very sudden and mysterious and, well, shocking. I'd figured yours for one marriage that would go on forever."

She gave me a curious glance, but my divorce wasn't something I wanted to discuss, even with Carol Lujan, so I let the conversation lapse. We spent a couple of hours in Albuquerque picking up a telephoto lens she'd located by phone, and some other stuff she needed, and a bite of lunch. It was well after noon when we hit the road again, so we didn't make it out of New Mexico that day. There was no hurry anyway, as Carol pointed out. She'd agreed that the best plan was for us to wait for another incident and make a dash for the scene—but until the saucer-men struck again, we didn't really know where we were going.

We stopped for the night in Lordsburg, therefore, down in the lower left-hand corner of the state. It was a typical western community with the Southern Pacific railroad tracks on one side of the main drag, and most of the town on the other.

After checking us into a motel, I left Carol to take a shower, and drove her car to a nearby filling station to be serviced. She was a nice girl—at least I hoped she was, Mac's suspicions notwithstanding—but the sticker on the door said she was as casual as most women about little things like grease and oil, and I didn't want any trouble south of the border where mechanics are scarce and auto parts scarcer.

It was dark when I returned to the motel. When I knocked on the door, Carol's voice said for me to come in, it wasn't locked. I found her, in a short white terry-cloth robe or beach coat, sitting on the floor at the foot of the bed with an open attaché case beside her and a lot of papers scattered around her, one of which seemed to be a map of Mexico. She looked up as I entered.

"It's no use," she said disgustedly. "I can't make any sense of these sightings. The things just seem to pop up— or down—all over northwestern Mexico, without any pattern or reason or anything."

I went over to the dresser to put down the cardboard icebucket I'd filled from the machine near the office. Again, the skeptical attitude seemed indicated, and I said, "Look, just between us, doll, do you really believe in these gadgets?"

Carol looked up, startled. "Flying saucers? Why, of course I believe in them! After all, we saw one once, remember?"

I shrugged. "Well, we saw a funny-looking green light moving across the sky, sure. But don't let's build it up to include any whirling discs piloted by little cheese-eating moonmen. All we saw was a light. Just a light."

"Matt Helm, do you mean to tell me you think this is all a wild-goose chase…?" She stopped abruptly. "Oh, I see," she said in a different, softer voice. "I see. Of course."

"What do you see?"

"It's security, isn't it? You're not allowed to admit that you know anything about it. Isn't that it?"

I looked at her for a moment, and put a grin on my face. "Sweetheart, you're way beyond me. Who's supposed to be telling me not to talk about what?"

"The people you work for, of course," she said calmly. "I mean the people you work for *really*, not that imaginary public relations outfit you talk about so unconvincingly." When I didn't say anything, Carol rose and belted the terry-cloth robe more closely about her, which was perhaps just as well, since it had become interestingly obvious that she wasn't wearing anything else. "Matt, let's stop pretending. Don't you see, I *know*. I know all about you. I've known for years. I know why Beth left you. She told me. She cried on my shoulder, when I came back from New York that time, and told me all about it."

"Just what did she tell you?" I asked.

"She said that before you were married you'd worked for a secret government organization, an organization that sometimes... sometimes killed people. I don't know how she found out about it. I mean she didn't go into detail, and she was pretty hysterical about the whole thing. We all knew how Beth felt about killing anything. She thought just hunting birds and animals was terrible. She couldn't face the thought that her husband had ever been in the business of... of hunting men."

I looked at Carol for a moment longer; then I grinned again and said, "Wow! On that, I need a drink. How about you?"

"Please."

Bartending, I went on easily, "Are you sure it was the U.S. government I was supposed to be working for? She didn't make me out an enforcer for the Syndicate, or a hatchet man for the Tongs?"

I turned to put a glass into her hand. She was watching me steadily. "Are you denying it, Matt?"

"Denying it?" I said. "Hell, no! I always wanted to be a dangerous gent with a shiv up my sleeve and a gat under my armpit. I think it's great. But if I'm such a terrible guy and you've known it for years, why did you fall on my neck when you saw me this summer? It doesn't seem to me you're taking my ex-wife's melodramatic tale very seriously, yourself."

Carol's eyes didn't waver. "I'm not Beth, darling. What do I care how many people you've killed?"

Her voice was a little defiant, as if she were reassuring herself as well as me. There was silence after she'd finished. Outside, we could hear the big trucks going past on the highway, heading west to Tucson, Arizona, and east to El Paso, Texas; but inside the motel room there was hardly any sound at all.

"I guess I'm being forward and unladylike," Carol went on at last. "But… well, it gets lonely. I wasn't really cut out to be a career girl, Matt. And I kept remembering a pretty nice guy who'd once held my hand and wiped my nose when I was in trouble, a guy who was now legally available. And then I went down to the bank one day and there he was. So I fell on his neck, like you say." She moved her shoulders, a little awkwardly for her. "What it amounts to, darling, is that you've had your month's free trial. Now you'd better start making up your mind as to whether you're keeping the merchandise or taking it back to the store. And in the meantime—" She stopped, and smiled at me, no longer awkward, and deliberately unfastened the robe and let it fall open. "In the meantime, you can practice making up your mind by telling me if I should put on some clothes so we can go out to eat. Or… or do you perhaps have some other ideas you'd care to put into effect before I get all done up again in girdle and stockings?"

Somehow we never did get around to dinner that evening. In the morning, we read in the newspaper that the fire-breathing UFOs had once more made hostile contact with earth, near a little Mexican fishing village named Puerto Peñasco, on the Gulf of California.

13

We entered Mexico by way of a town that was called Lukeville above the border and Sonoita—or Sonoyta—below. It was located on the section of the international boundary line between Arizona and Sonora that angles kind of northwestwards, eventually striking the Colorado River not too far above the point where it empties into the head of the gulf that the Mexicans like to call the *Mar de Cortez*, the Sea of Cortez: that desolate, rather narrow body of water almost a thousand miles long that's bounded on the east by the Mexican mainland and on the west by the Baja California peninsula, the long, dangling tail of the North American continent.

There wasn't a great deal of international traffic when we drove through the gate, so we were soon taking our turn at the desk inside the shabby little one-story customs-and-immigration building, watching one of the Mexican border officials making out our tourist permits. They have a dramatic, rapid-fire typewriter technique that's worth watching. Then we were on the road again, heading towards the village of Puerto Peñasco, some sixty miles away.

I heard Carol, beside me, give a funny, relieved little laugh as we left Sonoita behind and struck out across the cactus-studded desert at a legal one hundred kilometers per hour—sixty mph to you.

"What's funny?" I asked.

"Borders always scare me," she said. "I'm just a hick at heart. Matt?"

"Yes?"

"You're using me, aren't you?" She made a face. "No, don't make any sexy, double-meaning cracks, and don't tell me how you are just a poor little public-relations boy trying to get along in the big cold world. You've got some idea that I can be helpful to you down here in Mexico, don't you? Maybe you figure you'll attract less attention as a lady photographer's assistant, or something. Well, I just want you to know that I don't mind, so you can stop feeling guilty about it. Remember that I didn't *have* to invite you along just because you gave me a very broad hint."

I said, "Carol—"

She went on unheeding, "In fact, I think it's kind of romantic and exciting, darling. Just let me know what you want me to do—in a way that won't compromise your precious security, of course!"

I glanced at her, sitting there with her nice blonde hair and neatly lipsticked mouth and fresh complexion, thinking it was kind of exciting and romantic to be associated, even unofficially, with a dangerous character like me. I started to speak and changed my mind. First of all, I was under orders not to confide in her, and secondly, when they get that notion, all the words in the world won't drive it out of them.

She was wearing a tan skirt and jacket, with a silk shirt or blouse in a lighter color I guess you'd call beige. The fashionably short skirt had big pleats front and rear, making it suitable for reasonably vigorous activity, and the sporty, bush-type jacket had all kinds of pockets— you half expected a few cartridge loops, African style.

It was kind of a movie-safari outfit that went with her romantic notions, made more so by the little suede boots she was wearing. However, except for the thin shirt, it looked fairly durable, and professional photographers do tend to go in for individualistic costumes at times, so I didn't really hold it against her. If male camera artists could sport fancy hats and capes, it wasn't really a crime for a girl to show up on the job in a bush jacket, particularly if she looked good in it, which she did.

"Just one question," I said. "Exactly how did you happen to get saddled with this UFO photo-assignment, anyway?"

"Oh, that." She laughed. "There wasn't any 'happen' about it. I'm a determined, husband-hunting girl, darling, and I didn't really think you meant to come back to me, when you left so suddenly. So I was going after you. I asked myself why a crack U.S. undercover operative would be rushed to Mexico at just this time—"

"You're still a victim of my ex-wife's vivid imagination," I complained, going through the security motions. "The truth is, she just couldn't bear to admit we got divorced because we couldn't get along in bed." I saw that Carol was smiling, totally unconvinced, and I went on: "Anyway, I didn't tell you where I was going."

"No, but you didn't make any great effort to cover your tracks, did you? And Santa Fe is a small town, and I happen to know the girl in the travel agency, who sold you the tickets. And the big thing in Mexico right now is UFOs. I figured if I got a job covering the story, I'd probably run into you down there, somewhere…"

In a way it explained one of the coincidences Mac had thought incriminating, but it didn't really prove anything. In fact, I tend to be rather suspicious of females who claim to find me irresistible. It happens in this business, but the record shows that most of the ladies involved have ulterior motives for flattering me thus—a disillusioning fact that does terrible things to my ego.

Any woman, therefore, who uses my personal magnetism—or my matrimonial desirability, for God's sake!—as an excuse for chasing me the length of Mexico, or even laying plans in that direction, will normally find her explanation received with a certain amount of cynicism. But here, for no very good reason, I found myself believing in what I was told—or not so much in the story, perhaps, as in the girl who was telling it. I had learned nothing that would convince Mac of her innocence, of course; but I'd never been sold on the idea of Carol Lujan as a desperate communist agent in the first place…

I guess I was concentrating more on my thinking

than on my driving. At any rate, I almost ran us off the road when a horn blared, it seemed, just behind my left ear. I pulled aside and let a big black U.S. made sedan shoot by: one of those mean-looking front-wheel-drive Oldsmobiles with concealed headlights. Detroit has got very bashful about its light-bulbs lately. They get some funny notions of propriety in that town. A few years ago, if I remember correctly, it was the tires and wheels that had to be decently covered, with modest little skirts that made it almost impossible to change a flat.

The car was driven by a dark-faced individual wearing khakis and an official-looking cap. I didn't know him, but the front-seat passenger was a well-dressed Mexican gentleman with a neat moustache that looked very familiar. I'd last seen it in a hotel room in Santa Fe. Apparently our friend Solana-Ruiz also read the morning papers—or maybe he had private sources of information. In any case, he apparently considered the Puerto Peñasco incident worthy of his personal attention. He had to be going there since the road went nowhere else.

A woman was riding in back, but I couldn't get a good look at her through the dark glass. Nevertheless, I had an uneasy feeling that under more favorable circumstances I might have recognized her, although at the moment I couldn't think of any female acquaintance Mr. Solana and I might have in common.

"What's the matter, do you know that man?" Carol asked.

"What man?"

Carol laughed tolerantly. "You're very stubborn, aren't you, darling? I'm just going to have to learn not to ask any questions at all. How much farther do we have to go? I thought it was only sixty miles from the border. It doesn't look as if you could find a cup of water in this wasteland, let alone a whole gulf of it."

We came upon the town almost without warning. The character of the landscape didn't change much, but suddenly there were some dark objects on either side of the straight, paved road ahead. Reaching them, we discovered that they were mud houses, and that we were at the outskirts of Puerto Peñasco. Half a mile farther, and we could see the water ahead: a blue bay with a sandy beach curving towards a rocky point sticking out to the left, where most of the town seemed to be located. There were docks and warehouses and a number of sturdy-looking fishing boats.

The place that had been recommended to us by an Arizona filling-station attendant who'd been there was called the Motel Playa Hermosa—the Beautiful Beach Motel. We turned off at a big sign before reaching the town proper, and bounced along an unpaved street leading to the beach. The motel area, on the waterfront, was enclosed by a wall, inside which we found a number of low buildings and a larger structure housing the office, restaurant, and bar. Driving up to this, I saw Solana-Ruiz's Oldsmobile parked in front, looking like a blind monster from the ocean depths—or maybe it was just taking a nap with its eyes closed.

Several tables on the veranda by the front door were occupied. At one, a girl sat alone. She was wearing very snug, ankle-length, elastic pants, kind of orchid in color, and one of those skimpy sleeveless white jerseys that look like a man's undershirt. It bulged in an interesting way although she was not, in other respects, a bulgy girl. She had thick lipstick on, and heavy eye-makeup. The elaborately formal arrangement of her piled-up brown hair contrasted oddly with the scanty informality—if that's the word—of her costume.

I didn't look at her too hard. In the business, it's considered impolite to recognize people you know until they've indicated that they're willing to be recognized. I looked just long enough to make quite sure that this bosomy tight-pants chick was really my slim vestal virgin from Mazatlán, the sweet young girl who'd called herself Priscilla Decker.

As I started past her Priscilla looked up and said, clearly, "Well, if it isn't the super-spook himself! What are *you* doing here—as if I didn't know!"

14

Carrying the suitcases into the unit that had been assigned to us, I was surprised at the icy sharpness of the wind off the gulf. I remembered the sweltering heat of Mazatlán, only a few hundred miles south on the same coastline— well, seven or eight hundred. Apparently the weather had changed drastically during the couple of days I'd been out of Mexico.

I set the bags down and went over to investigate the primitive gas heater set into the wall. The room was just a cinderblock cell, gaudily painted and cheaply furnished; and like any beach house in autumn, it had a damp and clammy feel. I felt Carol come up to stand behind me.

"Matt, what's a spook?"

"I believe the word is a colloquialism for ghost or disembodied spirit, ma'am," I said without looking around.

"But it's also slang for intelligence agent or spy, isn't it?" Carol laughed softly. "She really let your cat out of the bag, didn't she?"

I turned the valve, applied a lighted match to the outrushing gas, and closed the battered cover of the heater. "I've never seen the dame before in my life," I said. "It was a simple case of mistaken identity. You heard her admit it."

"Of course, darling. There are so many men six-feet-four running around these days, you just can't tell them all apart."

I got up and turned to face her. She looked at me for a moment, smiling; then her smile died, and she reached out and touched my cheek with her fingertips.

"I'm sorry. If you aren't allowed to tell me anything, you aren't, and I shouldn't tease you. Matt, do you love me? Or is that classified information, too?"

I made the standard response to that ancient question. I took her into my arms and kissed her hard. Her lips were warm and responsive, and as I held her I couldn't help the thought, that comes to us dangerous gents from time to time, that it would really be pleasant to have an understanding woman to come home to between assignments—particularly if the understanding woman were blonde and lovely and nice to be with like, say, Carol Lujan. After a little, she held me off gently.

"That's not… not answering my question!" she said, rather shakily.

I grinned. "Why are women always so dead set on having it put into words?"

"Maybe—" She licked her lips, looking up at me. "Maybe because they're afraid. I'm scared, Matt. I've got a funny feeling... I don't like this place. I don't like that girl on the veranda. It isn't really going to be romantic and exciting, is it? All right, all right, I know you can't tell me anything But I wish we could just turn around and drive back across the border to that nice motel in Lordsburg and forget the whole thing." She laughed abruptly. "There! I've got it off my chest. Now I'll let you wander over to the bar for a beer, or something, while I rinse the alkali dust off the face and body."

I looked at her suspiciously. "Why the sudden modesty?" I asked. "I'm a big boy now. I've seen girls undress before, present company included."

"You're being stupid, darling." Her voice was a little sharp. "Don't you see that I'm giving you an opportunity to make contact with your fellow-agent without my embarrassing presence? Run along now like a good little spook. Shoo. Scat!"

The late afternoon sunshine struck me as I stepped outside, but so did the wind, making me wish I'd taken time to grab a sweater or jacket. I walked along the low wall separating the motel compound from the beach. Down at the shore, some kids were playing in the breaking waves. I noticed that several of them were wearing those black-rubber wetsuits for warmth. I didn't blame them. It wasn't exactly what I called ideal swimming weather. Other kids were setting off the usual Mexican firecrackers. A couple of beach buggies were racing around on the sand: stripped-down Volkswagens, by the look of them, with little open bodies and big tires.

I turned into the bar, which wasn't crowded, and found myself a stool without really looking around.

"*Una cerveza, por favor*," I said in my best Spanish, which isn't very good. I was aware that somebody was taking the seat to my left, and I caught a whiff of cheap, strong perfume. "Make that *dos cervezas*," I said.

"How do you know I want beer?" Priscilla Decker asked.

"If you don't want it, I'll drink both of them, and you can buy your own damn booze," I said. "God, you stink! What is that stuff you've got on, insect repellent or varnish remover? And just what the hell are you and that smoothie boss of yours trying to pull now?"

"What do you mean?"

I put some American money on the bar, and tasted my beer judiciously. After the long, dry drive it tasted very good, but then, beer is something they always do very well down here.

"You know what I mean, sweetheart," I said. "Blowing my cover, such as it was, by greeting me like a long-lost friend!" She started to speak, but I went on: "Okay, if that's the way you want to play, that's the way we'll play it. But let me just remind you of the last time you and your clever chief and your smart colleagues tried to get tricky with me. Think hard, doll, and maybe you'll recall a hotel room not so far from here, and a short-haired lady whose costume consisted mainly of a mannish pantsuit and three bullets in the chest. Concentrate, Decker. I'm sure it will all come back to you if you concentrate."

Priscilla's eyes were narrow. "Are you threatening me?"

I grinned without humor. "You're goddamn right I'm threatening you! Just take your choice. Either we're working on this job together, or I'm working on it alone and you're working against me. Just so I know. There isn't really room for any stupid interdepartmental feuds, but if you want one, I'll give it to you in spades. If so, just tell me: would you rather have the remains shipped to Leonard in Washington, or is the local cemetery satisfactory?"

She looked at me hard for a moment, with anger burning brightly in her eyes. Then she picked up her glass and drank. When she looked at me again, the anger was gone—well, gone or skillfully concealed.

"Okay, Matt," she said quietly. "Okay, you've made your point. And of course you're right. We've been instructed not to like you, and to conduct ourselves accordingly."

I said, "Jesus Christ, are you working for your country or just helping some jerk in Washington play musical chairs?"

"I know," she said. "I know how you feel, and I feel the same way. But after all, he is my boss." She shrugged and held out her hand. "But let's call it a truce, just between you and me, Matt."

"Sure."

I took her hand, which was small and firm, and looked into her eyes which were warm and friendly now. They almost made me ashamed of my boorish outburst—which was, of course, exactly what they were supposed to do.

I grinned, and flipped my fingertips lightly across the front of her skimpy jersey. "You can help me decide a bet with myself," I said. "Is it Kleenex or compressed air?"

She laughed. "What makes you think they aren't genuine, sir? Oh, of course, you saw me without them, didn't you? I was really a rather naive and underdeveloped little girl in Mazatlán, wasn't I?"

"What's the theory behind this getup?"

"Don't be obtuse. We'd like the inside track with Señor Solana, naturally. And Mexican gentlemen, even very respectable Mexican gentlemen, make a kind of cult of virility, and seldom turn down an obvious challenge."

I grinned. "Well, you're obvious enough. Is it working?"

"Don't rush me. After all, I just got out of jail, changed my clothes and hairdo, and came racing up to the border to meet Solana and thank him for interceding in my behalf. That was when the news of the latest incident came through. He wasn't really planning to bring along a U.S. observer on this trip, but he did. So I guess you can say it's working pretty well, even though I haven't had time to get myself seduced yet."

"Have you been out to the scene of the interplanetary crime?"

"Of course not. We just drove in a few minutes ahead of you, remember? But Solana's promised to take me as soon as he's gone through some formalities with the local authorities."

I said, "It would be nice if you got me and my camera girl included in the invitation."

"Is that what she is?" Priscilla made a face. "Well, I don't know why I should do your snooty blonde any favors. And I'm not nice, particularly not to large bullying gents who threaten to kill me." She laughed at my expression. "All right, Matt. I'll see what I can do." She hesitated, and went on: "Don't tell Mr. Leonard, but I'm really kind of glad you're here. This job could get too big for one girl to handle alone. Solana seems to think things are coming to a head fast. Whatever we do, it had better get done in the next day or two."

"Sure," I said. "Well, I'm probably supposed to try to beat you to whatever it is and grab all the credit for my team, but under the circumstances I think we can work out a compromise if you're willing. Let's first take care of the heavies from heaven, and worry about the characters in Washington later."

"It's a deal," she said. "And I will talk to Solana, I promise."

15

She was as good as her word. I'd barely had time to get back to the room and wash my face and dig a windbreaker out of my suitcase and tell Carol as much as was good for her to know when there was a knock on the door. I opened it, and there was Señor Ramón Solana-Ruiz, dressed pretty much as I'd first seen him, in his business suit, white shirt, and tie.

His shoes were polished to a luster that was quite commendable, considering the dusty surroundings. As a concession to the desert, however, he'd added a pair of sunglasses to his outfit—or perhaps he just liked the slightly sinister look the big, dark, curving lenses gave to his handsome Latin face. He bowed ceremoniously when I introduced him to Carol.

"It is a pleasure to make your acquaintance, Mrs. Lujan."

"You're very kind to let us come along," Carol said. "Will I be allowed to take some pictures, Mr. Solana?"

"By all means. Do you have much equipment? Perhaps you would prefer to follow in your car so you will be less crowded. We will go first to the hotel in town, if you do not mind. I want to question the surviving victim, a Mr. Gregory Henderson, from Los Angeles, California. He came down here to fish over the weekend, I understand."

"Was he badly hurt?"

"No, apparently he just received some minor burns when he tried to rescue his wife, who died in the fire, but of course the experience was a great shock to him. We will talk with him first, and then we will drive out to examine what is left of his vehicle and camper—that is the name given to those housekeeping units designed for mounting on trucks, is it not? Then, if you wish, you may accompany us to view the body, although I am told it is not a pleasant sight."

Carol winced, but said bravely, "I'd better cover everything while I have the chance. You never know what shots those crazy people in New York are going to want. Let me get some things together. I won't be a moment."

Solana watched her move away across the room. In spite of the impenetrable glasses that masked his face, it was clear that he was favorably impressed—and she did look kind of nice in her crisp safari suit, with a high-necked white sweater replacing, for warmth, the thin blouse she'd worn earlier. When she straightened up, loaded with gear, he hurried forward to help her carry the stuff out to the station wagon.

I followed behind them, and spotted Priscilla Decker

waiting by the cars. "Maybe you should have stuck to your nice-girl routine," I said to her with a grin. "Maybe obvious challenges aren't what turn Mr. Solana on."

Priscilla laughed. "That's all right. He can carry her cameras all he wants, just so it's my fanny he pinches." She shivered slightly, and started to put her arms into the sleeves of the quilted jacket she'd been wearing over her shoulders like a cape. "My God, that wind is like ice! And here I thought I was coming to another tropical paradise like Mazatlán!"

I helped her on with the jacket, which looked like a stray from the ski slopes. It was the same lavender, or orchid, color as her skintight pants.

"And I was congratulating myself on finally having promoted a car with air-conditioning," I said wryly. "Incidentally, thanks."

"You see, I keep my promises," Priscilla said. "I hope you do, too... partner."

Puerto Peñasco proper turned out to be a much smaller and more primitive community than Mazatlán, with narrow, twisting, unpaved streets fighting their way through cracks between the mud houses. The adults didn't look very prosperous; and dirty, barefoot kids were everywhere. I reminded myself that shoes and baths are not really essential to a child's happiness; as a boy, I'd avoided them myself whenever possible.

The hotel, in the center of town, was a rather impressive stone building. Even the interior walls were stone, so that the hallway down which we were led resembled a tunnel through a mountain of masonry. A man in khakis was waiting for us. He had a holstered automatic pistol at his hip. He ushered us into Gregory Henderson's room, and left us there, returning to his post outside.

The small room, with its heavy stone walls, had the atmosphere of a cave, or a monastic cell, but the occupant was obviously no hermit or monk. He was sitting on the edge of the bed, wearing cheap, gaudy pajamas that had presumably been obtained for him locally. His hands were bandaged, and his face had an odd, pink, staring look: apparently he'd managed to scorch the skin a bit and burn off most of his eyebrows and lashes.

He was a young man in his middle twenties with an unfortunate resemblance to another young man I'd met recently: the streaky-blond beach-boy character calling himself Tony Hartford, who'd got himself shot by Harsek. The young man on the bed didn't really look much like Tony, being bigger and darker, but he did have something of the same self-conscious, hair-combing, mirror-watching good looks, only slightly marred by fire. I was surprised that he'd been brave enough to get himself burned at all, but then I'm prejudiced against the species. After all, Tony had apparently been brave enough to get himself shot. I don't suppose there's any real reason to think a man must lack courage because he fusses with his hair.

Henderson did it now, smoothing down his wavy dark locks automatically as he rose and reached for a cotton robe on a nearby chair, and stuck his feet into a pair of huaraches that looked very stiff and new.

"Maybe *you* can tell me when I'm going to get some clothes to wear," he said aggressively to Solana. "All my stuff was burned, you know. Your people here keep promising to scrounge me up something, but it's been a typical *mañana* operation so far. Always clothes tomorrow, never clothes today. I'm getting damn tired of lying around in pajamas, particularly these pajamas. My God, they're so loud they keep me awake when I try to take a nap!"

Solana said smoothly, "The haberdashery facilities of Puerto Peñasco are rather limited, señor, but I will see what I can do. I hope you are feeling better."

"I'm all right. What do you want, and who are all these characters? I'm beginning to feel like a monkey in a zoo."

"I apologize for the intrusion. Mrs. Lujan, Miss Decker, Mr. Helm, Mr. Henderson. Mrs. Lujan is a magazine photographer, señor. She would like some pictures, if you don't mind, but first I would like you to tell us what happened last night."

"I've already told your boys—"

"I have read the report of the local authorities, señor. However, there were certain language difficulties, were there not? I would prefer to hear it from you, so I can be sure there are no errors of translation. The incident took place in the evening, just after dark, did it not?"

"That's right. We'd been out fishing—we'd trailered our boat down here from L.A.—and we came in late. Edie warmed us up something for dinner…"

"That is your wife, Mrs. Edith Henderson?"

"That's right. Except you're using the wrong tense, aren't you?" Henderson's voice was bitter. "Whatever kind of things you've got flying around down here, they fixed Edie, damn them! They almost fixed me, too."

"They? You saw more than one flying object?"

Henderson drew a long breath. "No. I guess I was… well, hamming it up a bit. There was only the one. That was enough. That was plenty!"

"Please tell us what happened."

"Sure. Edie was doing the dishes. She told me the garbage can was full, would I empty it so we wouldn't have to smell it all night. I said sure, and took it out to where we'd dug a pit, out behind the camper. I dumped the can and was kicking some sand over the stuff when I… well, I just kind of *felt* this thing up there. I mean, it wasn't making any noise or anything, but I looked up and there it was, coming in from the east, inland. The sun was down by now, but the sky was still light, and I could see it plainly, kind of in silhouette, if you know what I mean."

Solana said, "Can you give us a description?"

Henderson shrugged. "Like I say, it was just a silhouette, kind of flat and round with a dome thing on top, say like half a marble sitting on a fifty-cent piece. Well, the main hull, if that's what you call it, was thicker than that and kind of tapering towards the edges, but that's the general idea."

"Were there any markings you could see, señor?"

"No." Henderson shook his head positively. "It just looked black to me, against the sky. I couldn't tell you the color, or markings, or anything like that."

"And it made no sound?"

"That's right. I started back towards the camper to call Edie out so she could see it, and then I realized it was coming straight at me, getting bigger by the second. It was fast as hell; it was on top of me before I knew it. I thought it was going to hit me, and I threw myself face down in a little wash or arroyo. I don't mind telling you I was scared. Then there was a kind of whooshing noise, and all the heat in the world, and I scrambled up to see the camper burning. All I could think of was Edie, and I tried to get in to her, but I couldn't make it." He looked down at his bandaged hands. After a moment, he went on: "There was a little explosion inside and it set my clothes on fire. I had to throw myself down again and roll around to put it out, and while I was doing that, the whole thing blew like a bomb. Maybe it was the butane tanks letting go, or something. I don't know. I... I don't remember much else."

"Then you did not see the actual attack," Solana said after a little pause. "You cannot say what kind of weapon was used."

"No, I told you. I was flat on my face in the arroyo. If I'd thought Edie was in danger... But it came at me so fast, all I could think of was to duck."

Solana frowned. "Mr. Henderson, can you explain why this object picked *your* camp to attack?"

"Hell, no!" Henderson said. "Don't you think I haven't been wondering about that, myself? Of course, we were parked some distance from the rest of the camp. Like Edie used to say, you don't go camping to live in somebody else's pocket. At least we don't... well, didn't." His face was angry. "And now maybe you can tell me just what the hell is going on around here. And just what the hell are you doing to stop it? If innocent American tourists can't come to Sonora for a weekend of fishing without being attacked by mysterious gizmos from the sky—"

"Mr. Henderson, we are doing our best to deal with the problem," Solana said smoothly. "And in the meantime I will make sure that you are supplied with suitable clothes as soon as possible. Now, if you are willing, Mrs. Lujan would like to get a few photographs."

We didn't actually have to twist his arm. In fact, despite his shock and grief, we had a hard time getting out of there with some film left unexposed. He wasn't exactly camera-shy, is what I'm trying to say.

Outside again, we followed Solana's eyeless Oldsmobile out of town. It had a big, blunt rear end derived from current racing practice: the two-hundred-mph boys have discovered some aerodynamic reason for sawing their cars off short these days, and Detroit has climbed right on the bandwagon. Well, it beats the fins we had waving behind us a few years back.

The campground was a few miles north of Puerto Peñasco. It was reached by an unpaved road through the coastal dunes that gave us no real difficulties; but I had a hunch it was no place to stray from the beaten track without a jeep or beach buggy. The place was called Bahia Choya, and it turned out to be a crowded community of pickup campers and house trailers—

excuse me, mobile homes—situated on a blue, sheltered bay diagonally across which, far to the north, could be seen the shimmering white sands of what I guessed to be the real desert, the *gran desierto* at the head of the Gulf of California.

The bay itself was pretty enough, for that barren coast. The campground was something else again, cluttered and trashy. I have the old-fashioned notion that camping is something you do to get away from the crowd, and I could sympathize with the late Edith Henderson for preferring a location away from this outdoor slum.

We spotted the remains of the burned-out rig a short distance back in the dunes, and left the cars at the edge of the solid road, and went in on foot. The fact that Henderson's truck had made it didn't guarantee that our low-clearance passenger vehicles wouldn't bog down in the soft stuff. It had been quite an outfit, I saw; not just one of those little metal cabs you slip onto the ranch pickup after you've finished hauling hay to the horses, but a real traveling cottage mounted permanently on a one-ton chassis.

The interior of the camper unit was pretty well gutted, and the explosion had blown out the roof, door, and windows, and bulged the walls, leaving the blackened bed, stove, and refrigerator, and the half-consumed plywood cabinets, staring at the sky. I walked up thoughtfully and ran my finger along the ribbed aluminum of the side, where it was still bright and shiny. I was aware that Solana had come up beside me. His expression was masked by the large, dark glasses—shades, as we hippies call them.

"What is your opinion, Señor Helm?"

"Where was the body found?" I asked.

"On the bed."

I said, "Those little men from outer space are real ingenious, aren't they?"

"Sí, señor. That is my thought. What conclusions do you draw?"

"I'm no detective, and if I were, I wouldn't admit it here." I threw a glance towards Carol, busy with her cameras. "To her, I'm just an innocent bystander, an old friend coming along for the ride. At least that's the idea I'm supposed to be selling her."

"I will keep it in mind. As an old friend, do you mind if I ask her to have dinner with me?"

I glanced at him quickly. "You're a fast worker, *amigo*."

"I haven't asked yet."

"Go ahead," I said. "I'll solace myself with the lady in lavender. If you don't mind."

"Of course not." He smiled. "Tastes differ, señor. Personally, I find American women in tight trousers rather unattractive. I merely gave her transportation as a matter of international courtesy."

It was a good joke on Priscilla, after the pains to which she'd gone to render herself seductive, but I kept my face straight, and switched the conversation back to business: "Do you have a medical report on the body?"

"Not yet," Solana said. "The medical facilities here are limited, but I had a specialist flown in. I had a feeling

we might need him. He is working on it now. He has
instructions to be very thorough. I'm afraid we have not
been investigating certain aspects of these phenomena
quite as carefully as we should have. Perhaps we have
taken too much for granted." He glanced at his watch. "The
doctor should be finished by the time we get back to town.
I do not think there is anything else for us to learn here. I
will see if Mrs. Lujan has all the pictures she wants."

He went over to where Carol was changing film. She
looked up and asked him something, and he made a little
bow of assent, and posed by the blackened wreckage of
the truck while she worked around him with the cameras.
Priscilla was wandering around kind of aimlessly, as if
she wasn't especially interested in murder from the sky.
She came over to me.

"Do you think there's anything significant in the fact
that the victims were U.S. tourists, Matt?" she asked.
"Remember, the same thing was true in Mazatlán."

"With the addition of a couple of Mexicans running
the fishing boat, who also got clobbered," I said. "Well,
maybe it's a clue, but I think there have been plenty of
incidents involving only natives. Ask Solana."

"Señor Solana seems to be busy elsewhere," Priscilla
said dryly.

"Sure. He's asking my girlfriend to dinner. He has my
permission. I have his permission to ask you to dinner. All
the formalities have been complied with. What do you say?"

She was studying me closely. "Are you being clever,
Matt?"

"No," I said. "Not very. I'd just like to know what, besides the lady's undeniable charm, makes our mustached friend so eager for her company at just this point in the investigation. Okay?"

Priscilla was frowning. "You sound… you sound as if you weren't quite sure of your snooty blonde. Or Solana either."

I grinned. "The last time I was sure of somebody, really positive beyond a shadow of doubt, it cost me three weeks in the hospital… Well, well. It looks as if the Latin charm is working. I hope you don't mind riding back with me."

She watched Solana guiding Carol towards the Oldsmobile, and said a trifle grimly, "Well, it's obviously either that or walking, isn't it?"

I said, "Incidentally, I don't believe he really pinched your fanny. He says he finds American women in tight pants rather unattractive."

She stuck out her tongue at me, and got into the station wagon. We followed Solana's car back to town. When we arrived at the house doing temporary duty as morgue and laboratory, the doctor had completed his examination and tests. We were allowed to see the body, and it was no treat. We were informed that it was the body of a woman in her late thirties who had burned to death, all right—but only after ingesting enough chloral hydrate to knock out a horse.

While we were assimilating this information, a man came in, rather breathless, and reported to Solana in rapid-fire Spanish that came too quickly and softly for me to follow it. Solana gave him some orders and turned to us, looking grim.

"It seems that Mr. Henderson has disappeared, under circumstances that demand my attention," he said. "Will you be so kind as to escort the ladies to the motel, Mr. Helm?" He turned to Carol. "I am very sorry to have to withdraw my dinner invitation almost as soon as it was given, but you understand and forgive me, I hope."

16

The restaurant of the Beautiful Beach Motel was a smallish, unpretentious room across the lobby from the bar, with six or eight tables served by a single waitress, a pretty little girl in a full-skirted cotton dress who seemed to love her work. At least, something made her happy enough to sing, and after she'd taken our orders and brought us some beer to drink while we waited, we could hear her out in the kitchen, twittering like a bird.

"But I don't understand!" Carol said abruptly. "What in the world is chloral hydrate, anyway?"

I said, "It's vulgarly known as a Mickey Finn. Knockout drops, to you."

"You mean... you mean Mrs. Henderson was *drugged*?"

"Uhuh," I said. "The pink polka dot men from Mars are real tricky little fellows. They apparently slid down a ventilator or something, put the lady to sleep, and planted an incendiary bomb to keep her company. Then they were teleported or rematerialized back up to their hovering space ship, the one that looked like half a marble on top of a fifty-cent piece. At least that's what Henderson would like us to believe. Of course he undoubtedly hoped that, in a backward community like this, nobody'd spot the fact that his wife had been fed a chloral cocktail before she was incinerated."

Carol gulped. "What you're saying is that Henderson murdered his wife and made up the flying saucer story to cover up."

"First being careful to get himself mildly scorched to make it look good. That's the general idea."

Priscilla looked bored, as if she'd had all this figured out hours ago. Maybe she had. She asked, "What put you onto it, Matt?"

"Well, the guy himself wasn't too convincing, was he? And the camper had obviously burned from the inside. The outside, in several places at least, was bright and clean. Of course, the hypothetical UFO could have shot an intergalactic napalm missile or something down through the roof, but there wasn't any hole that looked as if it had been made from outside. Everything had blown out, not in."

"What about the bomb? If Henderson did it, what do you think he used?" Priscilla asked.

I said, "Well, if I were doing it, I'd just put a big saucepan of gasoline on the stove, over a low flame, and run like hell. Sooner or later—probably sooner—the fumes would reach the fire and go boom. What our Greg actually used is for the experts to decide. Probably he was fancier than that. Murderers tend to be more complicated than necessary."

Carol said, rather tartly, "For a public relations man, you seem to know a lot about bombs and murder, darling."

She was needling me, not entirely in fun, and I wondered what I'd done to annoy her. Then I realized that Solana must have mentioned that he'd cleared the dinner invitation with me, and no girl really likes to be passed from hand to hand, or man to man. Still, it was a childish reaction under the circumstances. She might have been bright enough to realize that I wasn't just getting her out of the way so I could make passes at another woman.

I said, "Oh, we image-makers get around. Anyway, it looks as if Henderson felt guilty enough about something to run out."

"But why did he do it?" Carol asked.

"You mean, why did he kill her?" I shrugged. "You heard the medical report. The lady was apparently in her late thirties, a good ten years older than her handsome husband. It makes a picture, doesn't it? Presumably she had money, money enough to buy him a fancy boat and camper rig, anything his virile young heart desired, but he preferred to have her dough without her company. Maybe he had somebody younger in mind to share the wealth with."

Carol shook her head dubiously. "Matt, you're just guessing!"

"Sure, but I'd bet on most of it. And it was bound to happen, with all these fatal UFO incidents being played up by the press. Somebody who wanted to get rid of somebody was bound to get the bright idea of ostensibly having them knocked off by a homicidal flying saucer. At least that's one possibility." I paused. "The other possibility is that he didn't just have the idea; that it was given to him."

There was a little silence. Carol frowned, not really getting what I was driving at. Priscilla started to speak, but was stopped by the arrival of the waitress with our food. We all waited until the little girl had served us and danced away, humming to herself.

"What do you mean?" Priscilla asked then, sharply. "Given to him by whom?"

I said, "Hell, I don't know. But it comes to mind, doesn't it? Suppose somebody picked this guy who had a wife he could do without—picked him and helped him to come down here and do the job, on condition that he blame it on a mysterious flying machine of a certain description. Why, it's a natural! Everybody gains, nobody loses, except Edith Henderson. Gregory gets rid of his marital encumbrance, and the Mexican flying-saucer myth gets another boost for the benefit of whoever's promoting it."

"Myth?" This was Carol, sounding offended. "Matt, you keep talking as if you didn't really believe in—"

I said, "I know, I know. You and I saw one once, with a couple of other witnesses along, all sober and reliable. Okay, but do you believe in *this* one? Do you believe in Henderson's Folly, and its whooshing weapon that sets things on fire from the inside, simultaneously pumping rich ladies full of chloral hydrate? And if this one is a phony, doesn't that make you kind of wonder how many other of these recent 'sightings' have been rigged? I may believe in flying saucers as a general proposition, but these particular Latin-American UFOs are going to have to put on an air show where I can see them, if they're going to convince me. I'm not buying any more second-hand reports from anybody."

Priscilla frowned. "What about that red-haired girl in Mazatlán? Do you think *she* actually saw—"

I coughed, and glanced significantly towards Carol. "I don't know what you're talking about, doll. You must be thinking of that other guy you keep getting me mixed up with, the super-spook character."

Carol grimaced. "Don't mind me, kiddies. Just go right on playing your cute little security games. But if this is all a hoax, who's doing it and why?"

"That," I said, "is the big question. Or perhaps I should say those are the big questions. And I can't answer them. Maybe Gregory can. And I find it rather suggestive that he's no longer available, don't you? He's out in the dunes somewhere, being chased by Solana's men, and ten will get you twenty they don't bring him back alive."

There was a little silence. Carol had a shocked look on her face. "Matt, what are you hinting at? Surely you can't suspect Mr. Solana—"

"Shhh!" said Priscilla quickly. She was facing the door. "Shhh, here he comes now."

We turned to watch him approach. It was dark outside by now, and he'd discarded the big sunglasses, but tonight his face looked no less remote and foreign with them off. There are times when you can kid yourself that men of all races and nationalities are basically identical; and then there are the times when the differences count for more than the similarities.

Tonight, obviously, Ramón Solana-Ruiz was a Mexican official on Mexican soil, and we were a bunch of lousy Yankee interlopers, a different and inferior breed of cattle. But he was still Latin enough to take a moment out for courtesy.

"I apologize again for being forced to desert you, Mrs. Lujan," he said to Carol. "I hope you had a pleasant dinner."

"Very nice, thank you," Carol said. "Mr. Solana, what about Gregory Henderson? Have you found him yet?"

Solana regarded her for a moment without expression. "There is a certain problem as regards Mr. Henderson. The gentleman seems to be armed. In making his escape, he shot to death the man I had left to watch him. One shot, señora, in the back. It was careless of the guard, of course, but at the time Mr. Henderson was not technically a prisoner."

"I was going to ask about that," I said. "How did you happen to have a guard on him in the first place? Did you suspect him right from the start, even before you came down here?"

Solana shook his head. "No, señor. I did not suspect him, not until after we'd had our little talk with him. He is not a young man who inspires trust, would you say?

Listening to him, I was fairly certain he was lying; the evidence at Bahia Choya pointed the same way; and the medical report confirmed it. But I had already given instructions to have him guarded, for the simple reason that these witnesses seem to be, shall we say, rather ephemeral. They do not seem to last very long. I wanted to be sure of preserving Mr. Henderson for interrogation. Unfortunately, I failed." He paused and looked from me, to Priscilla, to Carol, and spoke deliberately: "However, there are compensations. Once I have determined which one of you gave him the gun, I may be able to learn more from that person than I could have from Mr. Henderson."

I heard Carol gasp. Priscilla, being a pro of sorts, made no sound, and neither did I. Solana, still standing, looked down at the three of us bleakly.

"Let us understand each other, my *gringo* friends," he said. "Henderson was brought into town with his clothes half burned off. Nothing was brought with him but what was on him. His clothes were removed, he was treated for his injuries, and pajamas were provided for him, also a dressing gown and sandals. In other words, the man was stripped and thoroughly examined by a doctor, after which he was given new clothing and transported to the hotel. Such possessions as he had had on his person remained behind. If there had been a gun among them, he would have had no further access to it, and there was no gun. It follows that the weapon must have been smuggled into his hotel room after he was established there, by someone who came to visit him."

I said, "Henderson told us he was beginning to feel like a monkey in a cage. That would seem to indicate we weren't his only visitors by a long shot."

"True, Señor Helm, but I have just finished investigating all others who entered that room, and while it is not possible to be legally certain they can all be eliminated, I am morally certain that is the case. Remember, it was not just a matter of slipping a message on a scrap of paper from hand to hand. A gun is a fairly bulky object, not something the hotel maid, for instance, could readily have concealed on a plate of food, or under it. But it could have been concealed in a camera case, Mrs. Lujan."

Carol looked startled and indignant. "Really, Mr. Solana."

He went on as if she hadn't spoken. "And it could easily have been transferred to Mr. Henderson, señora, by you or one of your companions, while he was being posed for your pictures—the pictures he was so strangely eager to have taken despite his recent, sad bereavement."

I said, "Hell, that guy was a lens louse from the day he was born. You can't prove anything by that."

"Perhaps not, but the fact remains that of all the people who entered that room, you three were best equipped to smuggle in a pistol, and you had the best opportunity to deliver it to Henderson unseen." He looked down at Carol. "I regret this very much, señora, but I must ask you to consider yourself under arrest."

Carol's eyes were wide and shocked. "But you can't be serious! Why—"

"I am very serious."

"But why *me*?"

Solana sighed. "It has to be you, Mrs. Lujan, by a process of elimination. Whether or not you are aware of it, Miss Decker and Mr. Helm are both U.S. agents. Both were introduced to me by their superiors; there can be no possibility of mistaken identity. Treason is always possible, of course, even among the most carefully screened operatives, but in this case it seems unlikely. Both were given the highest recommendations. You, on the other hand, are an unknown quantity. Who vouches for you, señora? Does Mr. Helm?"

Carol turned quickly towards me. "Matt, for heaven's sake tell the man—"

I said, "You're making a mistake, Solana. I've known this lady a good many years. I'm sure she's okay."

Solana had turned to look at me intently. I had a hunch he was trying to tell me something. He said, "You speak in your private capacity, señor. Are you not willing to vouch for her officially?"

I looked at him for a moment, trying to read his expression. Then I glanced towards Carol, but turned back to Solana, since that was the more comfortable direction. Actually, of course, there was no real problem. Mac's instructions could have been tailored specifically for this situation. *You will maintain your cover story,* he'd said, *with a perfectly straight face even if circumstances conspire to render it totally ridiculous.*

Whether he'd been right or wrong in saying it, he'd

said it, and he was the boss. I'd acted on my own in Mazatlán and he'd backed me up. Now it was my turn to back him up by following his orders to the letter, silly though they might seem—and as a matter of fact, they kind of fit in with the vague plan to which I was working. Maybe they even fit in with the plan to which Solana was working, which seemed to involve getting Carol away from us, either by buying her a dinner or arresting her. What he had in mind, I couldn't guess, but I could try to find out.

I drew a long, harassed breath, therefore. "Here we go again," I said to Solana. "I've been telling the lady for more than a thousand miles, and now I'm telling you: I have no official capacity. I don't know who's supposed to have vouched for me—" I looked him in the eye as I said it. "—and I don't know why the hell you all want to turn me into a secret agent. I'm perfectly willing to give Mrs. Lujan the best character reference in the world, she's a wonderful girl, but when it comes to providing her with a security clearance..."

"Matt, really! You're running the gag into the ground. But if that's the way you want it...!" Carol got abruptly to her feet. She spoke stiffly to Solana: "Will you let me get a few things from my room before... before you take me away?"

"Of course, señora."

"Then let's go right now, if you don't mind!"

She marched to the door, very straight and dignified in her jaunty skirt and jacket, before Solana could respond either way. He glanced at us, shrugged, and followed her out. I heard Priscilla laugh a trifle maliciously.

"I don't think she likes you any more, Matt."

I said sourly, "Hell, even if I'd wanted to break cover, I couldn't have given her a clearance because she hasn't got one. Washington's still checking her out."

"Okay, but you could have said so. And what's with this cover bit, anyway? If you had a scrap of it left after my loudmouthed performance this afternoon, Solana just blew it for you. Who are you trying to fool?"

I said, "You, sweetheart."

She looked at me sharply. "What do you mean by that?"

I grinned. "Honey, I'm under strict orders not to give Mr. Leonard's people one single thing they can use against me in a security way. That means you, doesn't it?"

"Matt, you're being ridic—"

"Am I? My chief doesn't think so. Anyway, ridiculous or not, you will not catch me revealing secrets in front of any person unauthorized to hear them, even if they're secrets everybody knows, like the identity of one M. Helm. You can spill them, Solana can spill them, but my lips remain firmly sealed. I am a harmless publicity gent on vacation until I'm told otherwise."

Priscilla laughed and put her hand on my arm. "So that's the reason for the comedy routine! Well, maybe you're right, at that. Mr. Leonard would certainly like us to get something on you, after what you did to us in Mazatlán. Just between you and me, he's a vindictive, stupid little pipsqueak with an ego as big as a house."

I grinned at her. "What a way to talk about your employer!"

"Am I supposed to love him just because I work for him? Do you love the man you work for?"

I said, "Not exactly, but he's not a pipsqueak."

"So I hear. Incidentally, I don't quite get your strategy, partner. Are you really throwing the Lujan to the Solana, or are you by any chance throwing the Solana to the Lujan? Personally I never trust those healthy-looking, clean-looking, pure-looking blondes. Is she really a professional photographer? She looks—and acts—like a movie star just playing the part."

I said, carefully, "She's sold a few pictures over the years. Quite a few."

"But maybe that's not all she's sold, you mean?"

I laughed. "Don't put words in my mouth. Frankly, I'm betting Solana's the one to watch, but I wouldn't make the bet very big. We'll just have to let them sort it out between them and see what happens."

"Well, we don't have to do it here," Priscilla said, rising. "I've got some mescal in my room. That's the bottle with the pickled bug in it—the maguey worm, to show the stuff is made from the genuine maguey plant, whatever that may be. I haven't been brave enough to sample it yet, but with a little moral support from you—" She paused as I helped her on with her ski jacket, and glanced up at me over her shoulder. "Or even a little immoral support," she murmured.

I laughed, holding her lightly. "What do you think I am, Decker, just a butterfly flitting from flower to flower, from blonde to brunette? Hell, the love of my life has just stalked out that door, presumably forever. Give a man time to catch his breath."

She smiled. "You don't need much time. A few days ago the love of your life was lying dead on a hotel room floor, but you seem to have made a pretty good recovery from that passion. If we walk real slow, maybe you'll have caught your breath from this one by the time we reach my room. It's way up near the end of the compound."

I said, "You're a callous, disrespectful bitch. Just give me a minute to pay the bill…"

I left a generous tip for the little Mexican girl with the ready song. Outside, the wind still blew cold and sharp off the Sea of Cortez, carrying fine grains of beach sand with it. The leaves of the scattered palm trees in the parking lot rattled and clashed over our heads as we made our way towards the waterfront units in the dark, avoiding the black shapes of occasional parked cars.

Priscilla slipped a hand under my arm for support, as we fought our way along the buildings, buffeted by the wind. The other hand was trying to preserve her elaborate hairdo from total destruction. She stopped at a door and fumbled in her jacket pocket for a key, checked herself, and laughed.

"That's right, the lock doesn't work, like most things around here. Just open it, Matt."

As I opened the door, I had the sudden feeling I'd

seen this show before. There had been rain in that other scene and not so much wind, but this wasn't the first time recently I'd come to a woman's door by invitation on a stormy night…

"Just a minute. I'll get the light," Priscilla said, stepping past me to find the switch. I saw her recoil abruptly as the light came on to show the interior of the shabby room; then she'd thrown herself aside and down, shouting: "Matt, look out, he's got a gun!"

It was Henderson, in badly fitting work shirt and pants he must have stolen somewhere; and he had a gun all right, one of those tiny derringers that are just about as low as you can get on the firearms ladder. Still, they are compact, and as one U.S. president found out the hard way, they will kill. The one Lincoln met was, as I recall, a single-shot job; this one had two stubby barrels, one above the other. That was about all that could be seen of it. The rest was pretty well covered by Gregory Henderson's bandaged hand.

Well, I had a gun, too. After years of this work, you learn it's bad business to ignore your hunches. I'd been slow in Mazatlán under similar circumstances, but I wasn't making the same mistake here. I'd had the weapon drawn before Priscilla switched on the light—but another thing you get from experience is a feeling for when a man is going to shoot and when he isn't.

Henderson didn't have that cocked-and-ready, here-goes-everything aura. It was a dangerous gamble—my instincts aren't infallible—but we wanted the man alive and talking, so I held my fire, and he didn't shoot. We faced each other like that, at point-blank range, for a second that seemed much longer; then a gun crashed to my left and Henderson's knees buckled and he fell.

I looked at Priscilla, crouching in the corner, holding a short-barreled .38 revolver from which trickled a wisp of white smoke. Her face was white, too.

"Were you paralyzed or something?" she snapped. "He was going to shoot, couldn't you see it? Another second and you'd have been dead!"

I said grimly, "Considering the way your boss feels about me, I think it's wonderful the way you people keep saving my life."

"Well, that's a fine way to talk after—"

"That will do!" It was Solana's voice, behind me. "You will please throw your guns on the bed, both of you, and raise your hands!"

17

His voice said he had a gun, too. Everybody had guns in Puerto Peñasco tonight. I tossed mine on the faded coverlet—well, Vadya's: the little 9mm Browning I was still carrying. After a brief pause, it was joined there by Priscilla's .38 Colt.

Priscilla scrambled to her feet, and I moved over to join her, since it makes a man nervous to try to cover two people standing apart, and I had no designs on Solana's nerves at the moment. Later, a little psychological warfare might be indicated, but right now it was more important to learn what the man knew, and what he was planning to do about what he knew. It looked to me as if he had just made a great big mistake, moving in too soon when there was no reason for haste, but perhaps I was doing him an injustice.

He entered the room cautiously, holding a pocket automatic very much like my Browning, except that the workmanship looked Spanish or Italian rather than Belgian. It's hard to say what makes the difference, but it's there. Behind Solana was Carol, her blue eyes wide at the sight of death—her second such view that day.

Solana gestured us aside, and came forward to take the guns from the bed. Pocketing them, he stepped back again, and spoke to Carol without looking around.

"Come in and close the door, Mrs. Lujan. Wait over in that corner, please. If anything should happen, lie down on the floor; you will be safer there." His dark eyes seemed to be focused on a point halfway between Priscilla and me. "I sincerely hope that nothing will happen. There has been enough violence in this room tonight, don't you think?" His glance touched the dead man on the floor for an instant, and swung back to us.

Priscilla said quickly, "He was lying in wait for us, Ramón. He was going to shoot. We had no choice!"

"We, Miss Decker? I heard only one shot. Did you fire, Mr. Helm?"

"No, but—"

"Why not?"

I said, carefully, "Maybe I've had a little more experience along these lines than Miss Decker. I had a hunch he wasn't quite ready to throw the big, black dice. Besides, with that derringer, there was a good chance he'd miss if he did shoot. Those little things won't hit a manhole cover at ten feet unless the shooter's had lots of practice. I didn't think Henderson had."

That was a mistake. It's always a mistake to show any intelligence in a situation like that; it's much safer to act totally dumb.

Solana pounced: "What made you think so? I thought you did not know the man, except for your brief encounter with him at the hotel. How could you know anything about his marksmanship? After all, he did manage to kill a policeman with one shot."

"It must have been a lucky shot," I said. I indicated the derringer on the floor. "If he'd known anything about guns, to amount to anything, would he have come here with *that*?"

Solana frowned. "I do not understand. If that was the weapon that was smuggled to him—"

I said irritably, "Hell, *amigo*, use your brains. Your man, the one who got himself killed, had a great big .45 auto on his hip, didn't he? It was probably loaded with eight 230-grain slugs, real firepower. So why was this character running around with a lousy little .22 derringer holding two lousy little 40-grain loads, one of which he'd already fired? Why didn't he throw the toy away and grab a real weapon from the dead man's holster?"

Solana said, "I see your point, but—"

I went on without letting him finish: "It's only movie and TV actors who run off leaving effective firearms behind so they can have their rousing fistfights without being hampered by a lot of embarrassing hardware— actors with bad scripts, and people with very little experience, who don't think in terms of guns at all. When I saw that derringer, I knew that, murderer or no, he was just a scared duffer who didn't really want to shoot anybody else. If he'd had more killing in mind, he'd never have passed up the .45."

"I see your point, my *gringo* friend," said Solana. "But am I to believe that you reasoned all this out the instant you found yourself facing an armed murderer? That is very quick thinking indeed, señor."

I shrugged modestly. "And is it a crime to think fast in Mexico, Mr. Solana?"

He smiled thinly and didn't answer the question. Instead he said, "Very well. To sum up: you thought Henderson wouldn't shoot; Miss Decker thought he would. If he did shoot, you thought he'd miss; Miss Decker thought he'd hit."

I grinned. "Or you could say that I was willing to gamble a bit with my life and Miss Decker wasn't."

"Very humanitarian of Miss Decker," said Solana dryly. "If true. However, there is still another explanation for this difference in behavior. There is the possibility that you, Mr. Helm, were simply anxious to keep Henderson alive so he could talk; and Miss Decker was anxious to have him dead so he couldn't. The question then becomes: why should two U.S. agents have such different attitudes towards the same situation?"

I didn't glance at the girl beside me, who hadn't moved or spoken. Behind Solana, in the corner, Carol looked pale and scared. The door and windows rattled under the impact of the wind, but there was no other sound for a second or two.

Then Solana went on deliberately: "I must confess that I was not quite honest, back there in the restaurant. I did not spend the past hours investigating suspects. That is routine police work, and I am certain it is being handled quite competently by the proper authorities, who are also, I am sure, conducting the search for Mr. Henderson with great efficiency. Unfortunately, they do not have quite as much information as I have. They think they are dealing with an ordinary murderer. They do not realize that they are dealing with a man being used as a pawn in a game of international intrigue—a pawn that has just been sacrificed to protect a more valuable piece on the board. A queen, perhaps?"

Priscilla stirred at last. "I don't know what you're driving at—"

Solana ignored her. "Instead of assisting the police investigation, I have spent the past hours out in the dunes with a pair of night glasses, watching this room, assigned to Miss Decker, and the one in the next building assigned to you, Mr. Helm, and Mrs. Lujan. I wanted to learn to which one of you Henderson would come for help, when it became dark enough that he thought he could not be seen. He came here."

Priscilla said sharply: "That doesn't prove—"

Solana recognized her existence at last, looking straight at her. "No, Miss Decker, it does not prove that you were the one who gave him the gun, and presumably at the same time instructed him, by voice or written message, to make his escape and meet you here after dark. At least it does not prove that you were acting alone. Two United States agents in the same small Mexican town might well be working together, might they not. As a matter of fact I had reason to believe you were; I attended a conference at which both your superiors were present. However, I always like to confirm my suspicions before taking action."

He glanced at me, as if expecting me to comment; when I did not, he shrugged and went on: "If Mr. Helm were involved, he would not have wanted the murderer to appear at the room he shared with Mrs. Lujan, who apparently does not also share his secrets. He would undoubtedly have used this one for the rendezvous—Mr. Henderson's rendezvous with death."

Priscilla licked her lips. "But—"

"But if Mr. Helm had wanted Henderson dead," Solana went on remorselessly, "he would have fired the instant he was certain of his target. Instead, he refrained from shooting at some risk to himself. *You* are the one who fired, Miss Decker, to silence the man who could have betrayed you. I believe you invited Mr. Helm to your room just now, on one pretext or another—I won't ask what it was—hoping you could maneuver him into doing your grim work for you. When he balked, you did it yourself."

I glanced at Priscilla and she looked away. It occurred to me that I was getting a little tired of the legend of Triggerhappy Helm. So maybe I'd shot a little too soon once, in Mazatlán, did that mean I was going to commit everybody's homicides for them? First Harsek had tried to cash in on my hasty reputation, and now this kid had come up with the same tired idea…

Solana was looking at me again. He said, "I have already apologized to Mrs. Lujan for accusing her and pretending to arrest her. It was a necessary subterfuge to get her away from you and Miss Decker. I now apologize to you for my suspicions. I am satisfied that you are not involved in this scheme, although your country obviously is. I hope, since your superiors have seen fit not to give you a part in it, you will abide by their judgment and not interfere... Yes, Miss Decker?"

Priscilla had looked up. "How could I have smuggled a gun to Henderson?" she demanded. "*I* didn't have any camera cases—"

Solana's laughter cut her short. "My dear, it would be unchivalrous of me to suggest that your visible attributes are not entirely your own. However—" His glance touched the front of her lavender ski jacket. "However, when we get a matron to search you, I think we will find that certain improvements on nature were designed to serve a practical as well as an aesthetic function. It was a very small gun."

Priscilla flushed. She turned to me. "Matt, are you going to let this supercilious bastard—"

Solana said sharply, "Miss Decker, there is absolutely no point in your trying to draw Mr. Helm into your troubles. You are obviously a U.S. agent on a mission so secret that even your colleagues in other agencies have not been informed. Having met your chief, I can understand: he is a man who would want to keep the credit for his own organization. Well, let him keep the blame, too." He cleared his throat. "I admit I do not wholly understand the clandestine operation in which you are involved, señorita. I was deceived; I thought these flying objects were genuine, at least to the extent that they did exist and fly. Now it appears that some of them—perhaps all of them—existed only in the imaginations of the observers, and of Mr. Leonard's agents who hired or persuaded the observers to make their false reports. As the late Mr. Henderson was persuaded."

I said, "Look, you're jumping to conclusions, Solana. A lot of those reports mentioned U.S. insignia and uniforms, didn't they?"

"That was clever," Solana said coldly. "That seemed to indicate that the United States was being victimized— framed, I believe is the word. But now that I learn who is behind the plot, I wonder if these identifications were not part of a deliberate plan to create an atmosphere of menace throughout the northern part of my country, in preparation for a political or military move on the part of our great neighbor to the north."

I said, "Hell, man, you can't think we're going to *invade* you!"

Solana shrugged gracefully. "American troops have invaded Mexico before, señor. Exactly what demands will be made, I cannot guess, but it would be a cheap victory, would it not, if my government were to yield to the threat of a new U.S. weapon that did not actually exist?" He shrugged again. "In any case, the trial will bring out the details, I am sure. The fact is that a U.S.

agent has been captured in the act of conspiring against a friendly neighboring government. Please observe, Mr. Helm, that I am being scrupulously fair. I could arrest you as well, and make my case stronger by presenting two American conspirators—"

Carol moved. It was totally unexpected, at least by me, but obviously I'd underestimated her. She gave no warning, she made no speeches, she committed none of the usual beginner's errors; she simply stepped out of her corner and threw her arms around Solana from behind.

"Get his gun!" she gasped. "Oh, please, Matt, get his gun, quickly!"

18

A moment later I had Solana's automatic from his hand and the two guns from his pockets: mine and Priscilla's. I rearranged the arsenal so I could cover him with the weapon with which I was most familiar—the 9mm Browning—and nodded to Carol, who let go of him and stepped away, patting into place a lock of hair disarranged by the struggle.

"Sorry, *amigo*," I said to Solana. "Just one request. Please don't tell me I can't get away with it."

He made a little gesture with his raised hands, disclaiming responsibility. "It is your choice, señor Helm. I gave you an out, as you Yankees would say, because I believe that in your way you are a sincere and honest man. But if you wish deliberately to involve yourself in someone else's crime—international crime—you will have to take the consequences. As will Mrs. Lujan."

"Sure." I looked at Carol. "You heard the man. You just stuck your neck way out. Why?"

Carol licked her lips. "I... I'm an American citizen, aren't I? And while I think what that woman is doing here is incredible and perfectly horrible—what I understand of it—she *is* an American agent, isn't she? And I couldn't very well let Mr. Solana put her on display in a Mexican courtroom as proof of some sneaky kind of U.S. aggression, could I? I mean, we don't have to wash our dirty linen in public." She glared at Priscilla. "Not that it doesn't need washing badly!"

"I see," I said. "And as a patriotic American citizen, just what do you recommend as the next step."

"Why, get her back across the border fast!" Carol snapped. "Isn't it obvious, darling? Get her out of Mexico before there's a lot of dreadful and perfectly justified anti-American publicity. Without her, it's just Mr. Solana's word for what she was doing, and who's going to listen to a crazy story by one Mexican official who maybe hates the United States?" She glanced at Solana. "I'm sorry, Ramón, but I just had to do it!"

He smiled gently. "I see that now, señora. I should have anticipated it."

There was something just a little phony about the exchange. When you came right down to it, there was something phony about the whole performance, but this was not the time to determine who was being clever about what. Carol may have sensed the false note, because she went on quickly:

"When we get home, I'm going to find out just exactly what this is all about, and if it's really authorized by responsible people in Washington! I know some men who can find out for me, reporters. It looks like another one of those schemes the CIA is always being accused of, that I never really believed in before: intriguing and interfering in countries where we've got no business…"

I said, "Take it easy, doll. Save the political harangues. Right now we'd better get the hell out of here as you suggest… What do *you* want?"

Priscilla had moved up beside me. She was looking at me in a kind of expectant way. She held out her hand. "Why, I'd like my gun back, Matt."

I laughed at her. "You get back over there and keep your nose clean and your hands in plain sight. I don't like to be played for a patsy, Decker. Here or in Mazatlán or anywhere." I weighed the two extra weapons in my hand, slipped Solana's under my belt, and regarded hers with a frown before stowing it away. It was a reasonably portable firearm, as revolvers go, but you could hardly call it tiny. "You didn't have this stashed away in your falsies," I said. "Where did it come from?"

"I had it hidden under my pillow. Matt—"

"And just why do you need a gun right now?"

She shrugged. "Well, if *you* want to do it—"

"Do what?"

She glanced towards Solana. "Don't be silly," she said calmly. "Somebody's got to shoot him, don't they? Unless you know a better way of doing the job."

I heard a gasp from Carol. She started to speak, but I beat her to it. "There's going to be no more shooting here tonight," I said to Priscilla. "I'm getting awfully goddamned tired of you and your white-haired smoothie of a boss and your complicated intrigues. You're going back to the States and we're going to find out exactly what's what and who's who and we're going to do it without murdering a single additional Mexican citizen, male or female, official or unofficial."

Priscilla said coldly, "Since you put it so personally, Matt, I am getting very tired of you, too—of you, and your sanctimonious ways, and your fantastic habit of wrecking carefully laid plans that are none of your damn business. And I warn you, if you don't do exactly as you're told, your hide will be drying on a Washington fence just as soon as my white-haired smoothie of a boss can drop a word in the right ear." She jerked her head in Solana's direction. "That man must be silenced. He must not be allowed to report what he's learned here. Either you do the job or let me do it, but it's got to be done!"

I said, "Now that you've got all that off your chest, go over to that chair and sit down. And stay sat."

"Matt, I promise you, if you spoil this operation for us—"

"Yeah, I know. And I'll worry about my hide, later. Sit down!" I waited until she obeyed. "Carol."

"Yes. Matt, you're not going to listen to her—"

"Carol," I said without looking around, "please go to our room, get out my suitcase, and open it. There's a trick compartment…"

I told her how to get into the compartment, and what to

get out of it. She left, admitting a brief blast of wind and sand. Priscilla was sitting on her assigned chair, glaring at me, looking cheap and sullen and disheveled with her gale-damaged hairdo hanging over her ears in loops and wisps. I remembered the slim, pretty, virginal kid who'd met me at the airport in Mazatlán, and I couldn't help being reminded, a little, of Vadya, who'd had the same knack of tailoring, not only her costume and makeup, but her whole personality, to the character she was playing.

Well, it was a useful knack for anyone in our line of work, but I'd obviously underestimated Miss Priss from the start. I hadn't thought she was old enough, or experienced enough, to put on so good an act—whichever Priscilla was the act. Perhaps this tough, tarty girl was the real Priscilla, and the big-eyed innocent in Mazatlán had been the fake…

Solana stood in the middle of the room with his hands up. Despite the awkward position, he looked nice and relaxed, and maybe even a little wryly amused at his own predicament. There were some questions I would have liked to ask him, but not before witnesses—and particularly not before the witness we had—so I didn't ask. We just waited, and presently Carol returned with a small, flat case, which she gave to me after a moment's hesitation.

"Matt, you're not going to… to hurt him?"

I said, "Sure I'm going to hurt him. I'm going to stick a sharp needle into him, brutally, cruelly, without anesthetic, because I'm just a sadist at heart. Shove your sleeve up a bit, Ramón, and remember, I'm the guy who's keeping you alive. The lady over there wants you dead. So if you jump me, better make it good, because I'll throw her the gun if I can, and if she gets it she'll shoot, you know that."

I loaded the hypo I got from the little drug case. Solana watched me in silence. When I was finished, he asked, "May I inquire what you are planning to give me?"

"About four hours' sleep," I said. "You'll feel a little groggy when you wake up, but it'll wear off fast."

Priscilla stirred. "Matt, so help me, if you don't put him out for good—"

I said, "You were running this your way and you ran yourself right into a trap. Now I'm running it my way… Okay, Ramón. Whichever arm you prefer to have punctured. Swell. Now come on over to the bed and lie down, like a good boy."

Five minutes later he was sound asleep on the bed. I looked at the two girls, without appreciation. Not that I don't like girls, but this job had been overloaded with them from the start: Vadya, the blonde woman I'd shot, the red-haired girl who'd disappeared with Harsek, and Carol, who might originally have been classed as an innocent bystander, but was now as deeply involved as the rest of us, something I might feel guilty about later, when I had the time.

And, of course, there was the girl of many faces— well, at least two—who called herself Priscilla Decker, whatever her real name might be.

I said, "Okay, Priss. Now whistle up your magic carpet

and get us the hell out of here."

She frowned. "I don't know what—"

"Cut it out," I said. "It was arranged for you to come here in Solana's car, without any transportation of your own. It's an isolated Mexican fishing village, sixty miles from nowhere, served by just one desert road that can be blocked anywhere between here and the border. You had some dirty work to do, cleaning up after friend Henderson—maybe I should say cleaning up *on* friend Henderson—and it could go wrong, as it did. Don't tell me Leonard didn't arrange a back door of some kind for you. Well, now's the time to produce the key to that door."

She said sharply, "If you think I'm going to help you—"

I sighed. "Why didn't you say so before I put him out? Now we'll just have to sit here until he wakes up again and carts us off to prison." I glanced at Carol. "Pick a chair and make yourself comfortable. The girl's being stubborn. It looks as if we may be here for a while."

"Damn you!" This was Priscilla. "When we get back, I'll have your scalp if it's the last thing I do! And I don't know if there'll be room for all of us; I don't know how big a plane they've got standing by."

I said, "We'll worry about that when we see the plane. Where's it supposed to make the pickup, on the local airstrip I saw from the road?"

"Don't be silly, right there in town, practically? No, there's a place out on the desert just to the north where the highway runs straight for miles, roughly in the direction of the prevailing winds. We'll have to watch our steps; there may be a road block if they're still searching for Henderson." She glanced at the dead man on the floor without visible emotion, and looked up again. "Well, all right, damn you. Get me the radio stuff out of my suitcase and I'll make the emergency signal…"

Leaving the room, a few minutes later, I glanced back. Solana was stretched out on the bed, breathing evenly; but that wasn't what I was looking at. As I'd said earlier, it's only actors and amateurs who don't keep track of guns. I was checking on the little .22 derringer I had carefully neglected to pick up earlier, when I was collecting the rest of the armaments. It had been lying on the linoleum floor near the corner of the bed, but it was there no longer.

I grinned to myself, and closed the door behind me. Everybody was full of tricks tonight, even I. With a little luck, some of them might come off.

I put the girls into the front seat of Carol's station wagon, with Carol driving, and got in back where I could keep an eye on them. We drove out of town, switched off the headlights as we passed the last adobe shacks, and proceeded cautiously along the empty highway that led northwards to Sonoita and the border.

Presently we saw a gleam of light ahead, warning us of the expected road block. We turned off into the desert to make a wide swing around the spot. It was rough going, and pretty soon the wagon hung itself up on a hump between two gullies. These low-slung new vehicles appear very stylish on hard pavement, but they look kind of ridiculous stuck in terrain that any old pickup truck with reasonable clearance would take in its stride.

Rather than make a lot of noise trying to dig out, we just left the glamor-wagon there and continued on foot. Priscilla, impatient, forged ahead, which was all right with me. It turned out to be quite a hike in the dark. I plugged along beside Carol, and after a little she took my arm as if to steady herself, moving closer as we walked.

"Well," she whispered, "well, did I do all right, darling?" She laughed softly. "I'll admit I was a little slow to catch on. I even got a little annoyed when it looked as if you were trying to wish me off on another man so you could have the sexpot for yourself. But when... when you just sat there and let me be arrested, I realized that you *wanted* me to go with Solana for some reason. I hope I looked convincingly indignant."

"You did fine," I said. "I figured that since Solana seemed to want you so badly, he'd better have you; obviously he had something in mind. Now you'd better tell me just what was the purpose of the show the two of you put on... What's the matter?" I noticed that she was limping. "Did you twist your ankle?"

She laughed again, ruefully. "No, it's just the transmitter-thing Ramón gave me. I hid it in my boot, and it's rubbing a hole in my shin."

I said, "So that's his plan. He slipped you an electronic dingus to carry? A sending device of some kind?"

"Yes, of course. He's got it all fixed; they'll be able to track us wherever we go."

I made a face. "Well, it's not exactly an original idea, and I never trust those gadgets very far, but let's hope it works. Did he have any message for me?"

"Not really. I was just to grab him when he gave me the sign, so that you could overpower him, and we could all get away with *her*." Carol glanced towards the shadowy figure stumbling along ahead of us. "He hopes she'll lead him to the rest. To the headquarters or whatever it is, where they're getting things ready, he thinks, for some really big UFO demonstration that'll make all the others look silly. He says we haven't got much time, and he hopes you'll help. But, Matt, I don't understand. Who is this Mr. Leonard *she* is working for, and what kind of a U.S. agency would think of doing anything like this? I can't really believe—"

"Hold it!" I whispered sharply. "She's stopping."

Priscilla was waiting for us on a low ridge overlooking the highway. "I think this is the place," she said. "He ought to be here pretty soon; he's had plenty of time. Have you got the flashlight I told you to bring?"

I gave her the flashlight. We stood and listened. For a long time the night was silent except for the uneven murmur of the wind; then we heard the sound of a plane in the distance. Priscilla waited until it was overhead, and raised the flashlight, and sent some kind of a dot-dash message skyward. The plane circled away from us and came in over the dark ribbon of the highway, lower and lower. There was a chirp of rubber as its wheels touched the pavement and began to roll. We ran down the sandy slope to intercept it.

The plane had stopped by the time we reached it, and the pilot was already climbing out on the wing. He was a big, burly man, and there was something familiar about his head, even in the dark. Not his face, I'd never seen that before except in photographs, but I'd once seen that shaved bullet-head from behind, in a Mazatlán taxi piped for gas. I stopped abruptly, as if taken totally by surprise. Something touched me between the shoulderblades.

"As you say, it's not much of a gun," Priscilla said softly behind me. "But I don't really think you want to be shot by anything, even a .22 derringer… Did you have any trouble, Harsek?"

19

It was a moment of private triumph for me, and I should have felt real good about it. All my stray hunches and guesses had paid off, and my vague plans had worked out very well—it had been tricky, pretending to suspect everybody but Priscilla Decker so that she wouldn't guess I suspected her. It had taken some finagling, getting myself captured like this, and I should have been pleased at my success.

However, there were a few drawbacks to the situation. For one thing, I now had to survive until I was brought to the place where I could do the job I'd been sent to do, and that might be tough, particularly with Harsek around. For another thing, I wasn't alone in my predicament. I'd hoped Solana might keep Carol out of the action—that was one reason I'd let him take her away—but he'd used her as a decoy instead. I didn't blame him, it was the logical thing for him to do, but it gave me an additional responsibility I didn't need. I hoped his electronic tricks would make up for it, but I had no faith in them.

"I never have trouble, girl," Harsek was saying in a guttural voice. "Now get them aboard fast, before some *Mejicanos* decide to make use of their fine paved road."

"Just a minute. There's something I have to do first. Cover the man. Wait, let me give you his guns. We have quite a collection and I have no place to carry them... Okay." Priscilla swung around to confront Carol. "All right, honey, where is it?"

"Where is what?"

Priscilla regarded her for a moment, rather like an experienced cat appraising a very young and innocent mouse. Abruptly, she reached out with both hands, grabbed Carol's neatly buttoned bush jacket by the lapels, ripped it open, hauled it down from the shoulders roughly, and yanked it free of the arms. Priscilla kneaded the cloth thoroughly with both hands, feeling for something hard. Finding nothing, she threw it aside.

"Okay," she snapped, "step out of the boots, and take off the sweater and skirt, unless you'd rather have me pull them off you, too... Ah, I got a reaction, didn't I? It's in one of those ducky little suede boots, isn't it? Dig it out and give it to me!"

Miserably, Carol reached down and fished out a small object, which Priscilla snatched from her and threw far out into the dark. So much for electronics.

"You and your dancing partner really should have given your adagio routine a few more rehearsals," Priscilla said scornfully. "It wasn't as convincing as a lot of high school performances I've seen. So Mr. Solana thought he'd plant a tracking device on me, in the form of a ladylike blonde! What other cute ideas did he have in mind?"

Harsek said sharply, "This is all very interesting, girl, but we have an aircraft sitting on a public highway. We can question them later. Get them aboard."

I'm as brave as the next man, I hope, but no matter how much I ride in them, airplanes always scare me a little. Perhaps this is because I don't know anything about flying them except what little I've absorbed by watching other guys do it.

I can drive a car pretty well, and I've been checked out on horses, bicycles, motorcycles, skis, skates, and snowshoes; I can handle a boat in an amateurish fashion and I once managed to ride a surfboard without falling off; but the air is not my element. One of these days I'm going to take a few flying lessons so I'll at least know if the guy up front is doing the right thing or the wrong one.

In the meantime, crowded into the back seat of the little plane beside Carol, I didn't immediately do a lot of constructive thinking about our situation, although there was obviously a lot to be done. As far as I was concerned, the intensive cerebral effort could wait until Harsek got us the hell off that dark desert highway and up into the sky where we couldn't hit anything, at least not until it was time to come down again.

It took him a while. I've called it a little plane, and you could have checked it aboard a commercial jet and

had baggage allowance left over, but it still had two
engines and carried four people, which is a lot of plane
for a private job. With a full load of passengers, it didn't
really leap off the ground; and as we roared along the
shadowy blacktop fighting for takeoff speed, I expected at
any moment to see a car or truck appear ahead to contest
our right to the road.

There was nothing to indicate the exact moment we
stopped rolling and started flying. Harsek just reached
out and hit a switch and I heard the wheels come up, so
it seemed reasonable to assume that we were airborne.
When we'd achieved a safe margin of altitude, I cleared
my throat.

I said, "You drive this thing better than you did that
taxi in Mazatlán."

He was busy getting things trimmed and organized for
level flight. He said without turning his head, "It wasn't
much of a taxi. This is a good airplane. It is too bad that
we must lose it."

"Lose it how?" I asked.

"Never mind. You will see." He glanced towards
Priscilla, who sat half-turned in the right front seat so
that her revolver could cover us in back, particularly
me. Harsek said, "Give me a report, girl. You used the
emergency code. What went wrong?"

She said defensively, "I don't have to report to you,
Harsek. You are here to assist us, not to give orders
or conduct interrogations. I will make my report to
Command, when the assignment is finished."

"For a chicken that has just missed being plucked, if my guess is correct, you talk very bravely. But of course you are right." His voice was dry. "Harsek does not give orders here; he merely lends his well-known face and name to the operation. He also flies airplanes and drives taxis, and shoots guns if necessary. But the bright young children get the credit—and the blame, don't forget, if things go wrong."

"Nothing's gone wrong!" Priscilla said sharply. "Anyway, nothing serious."

"To be sure. Allow me to amend my request. Do not make a report. Merely bring me up to date, as one colleague to another. What situation did you leave behind in Puerto Peñasco? Since you did not bring him along, I assume you silenced that young man, the handsome, shifty-eyed one who wanted to kill his middle-aged wife for her money. It is really remarkable how many people can be found, if one looks hard enough, who are eager to commit a murder if only the blame can be placed somewhere else, even on beings from other worlds. Or did the man escape you? Is he now in the hands of the police, telling them about our project, as much as he knows? Which is not much, but enough to be damaging."

Priscilla hesitated. "He didn't escape; he's dead. However, there's a Mexican policeman or government agent, the man with whom I rode down there, who seems to have made some good guesses. I tried to have him killed—" She threw me an angry look. "—but I was not successful. But it does not really matter. No one will believe him. No one of consequence. Besides, he'll be unconscious for several hours, and his ingenious tracking device is lying back there in the cactus."

"So a policeman knows," Harsek said grimly.

Priscilla said, "I tell you, it doesn't matter! If we were dealing with military secrets, or technical data, it would be different, but we are dealing with flying saucers. It is a subject upon which people are not rational!" Either her vehemence, or the fact that she was talking to Harsek, who did not have to be deceived, had brought a faint accent to her speech. She went on quickly, "Let one Mexican government employee scream to heaven that these recently 'sighted' Mexican saucers are a hoax and do not exist, that all the latest reports from this area are total fabrications: no one will listen. No one, I tell you. The skeptics will remain skeptical and the believers will continue to believe."

"If you say so, girl." Harsek sounded unconvinced.

"I say so. That was the beauty of the scheme from the beginning. We are not dealing with scientific facts, we are dealing with a variety of religious fanaticism. Indeed, that is one of our problems. Even when we have demonstrated that all these individual deaths, and the final mass catastrophe, can be blamed on callous aeronautical experiments—perhaps even hostile military demonstrations—carried out by the United States over Mexican territory, some people will remain firmly persuaded that the real responsibility rests on creatures from Jupiter or Polaris, and that somebody is covering up the truth for reasons of policy."

Harsek shrugged his massive shoulders. "It is an interesting theory. Personally, I have the old-fashioned notion that secrets should remain secret, particularly from the local authorities, but as you have pointed out, this is not my mission. For your sake, I hope you are right."

There was silence in the plane for a while, as far as conversation went. The motors out on the wings were far from silent, however, and there were a number of small, constant, unidentifiable—at least by me—vibration noises. Presently I felt Carol grope for my right hand and grip it tightly. I glanced at her. Her white sweater and pale face were dim blurs in the darkness of the cabin.

"They're going to kill us, aren't they, Matt?" she breathed. "And Ramón can't help us now."

"They probably intend to. But let's not confuse intention with execution, doll. Can you fly one of these things?"

"What?"

"Can you handle a plane?"

She shook her head quickly. "Heavens, no! The few other times I've been up in little private jobs like this, I was scared half to death." She laughed wryly. "And people weren't even thinking about murdering me, those other times."

Priscilla, in front of us, shifted position irritably. "Be quiet. We have a long way to go, too long for listening to a lot of chatter."

The plane flew steadily on through the night in a

southerly direction, judging by the compass I could see past Harsek's head. Priscilla kept the muzzle of the .38 aimed at me over the back of her seat. It could not have been a comfortable position, but her attention did not waver as the hours passed. At last Harsek glanced at his watch, studied a map or chart briefly, and looked down through the darkness that was no longer quite as dark as it had been.

"The life preservers are in the rear," he said. "Get them out and put them on. We are about twenty minutes from our ditching point. Remember, do not inflate the preservers in the cabin or you will have difficulty getting through the door."

Carol found my hand again. I felt her fingers tighten fearfully. "You mean… you mean we're going to crash?"

"Not crash, Mrs. Lujan, ditch. I will put the aircraft down on the water in the shelter of a certain deserted little island down there. A boat is waiting to pick us up. There is no danger. The plane will float for several minutes. Miss Decker and I will disembark first, then you two from the rear. And, Mr. Helm, please remember that while we have adequate time to get out, if we work quickly, we do not have time for any foolishness. Don't be clever, unless you want to accompany the plane down into fairly deep water. Drowning is not a pleasant death, I am told. Now the life preservers, if you please."

We put them on awkwardly, in the limited space, and settled ourselves to wait some more. The sky was getting light to the left, now, and looking down I could make out that we were flying over water, presumably the same Gulf of California we'd known at Puerto Peñasco. I could see some ghostly islands far ahead, one kind of crescent-shaped; and near it was a small speck that might have been a boat. I leaned over to get a better look.

"Sit still!" Priscilla said sharply. "Harsek will do the navigating. Your assistance is not needed, Helm."

I grinned at her, and glanced at Carol, whose face looked pale and strained in the growing light.

I said, "Anyway, your question is answered, Carol."

She seemed startled at being addressed. "My question?"

"Back there you kind of asked if the lady was a real American agent working for a real American agency. The answer is: she isn't."

Priscilla laughed. "But I am! I am a very highly regarded operative of a fine new department run by the coming man of U.S. intelligence—an arrogant, handsome, ambitious, pompous nincompoop who knows nothing about our kind of work whatever. That is the great American fallacy, that there is such a thing as an administrator, per se, and that what he chooses to administrate is unimportant. Your schools are run by educators who know nothing of what is taught; your government is run by politicians who know nothing of governing; and now you commit the final absurdity of entrusting the delicate task of international intelligence to a pipsqueak who only knows how to outmaneuver other pipsqueaks for positions of administrative importance."

I grinned as she paused for breath. "Don't look to me for an argument. I don't like the guy, either."

Priscilla went on: "Planting a few agents on such a man, when he was building his organization, was ridiculously simple; and guiding him to the proper attitudes and actions was no more difficult, since he had no real grasp of what he was supposed to be doing." She laughed again. "Of course, I am telling this only to you, because you will not be repeating it to anyone. As far as the world is concerned, this vicious U.S. Air Force crime against Mexican sovereignty was only made possible by the ground activities of disciplined agents obeying the sinister orders of a fiendishly clever American spymaster."

I said, "Sure. Our undercover genius, Herbert Leonard. Well, it couldn't happen to a nicer fellow. I suppose some of those disciplined U.S. agents are going to get themselves captured by the Mexicans when the smoke has cleared, so they can spill the international beans."

"They will be captured or perhaps, driven by their consciences, they will defect in the next day or two after seeing the flaming horrors for which they have been responsible. And while you will disown them, as is the custom, you will not be able to do it very convincingly, since it will be well known in Washington that they were actually employed by an American agency."

I would have liked to ask more about the flaming horrors that were being planned for the next day or so—a mass catastrophe, she'd called it earlier—but she would probably have refused to answer a direct question on the subject, and I didn't want to stop our little chat while it was still producing valuable information.

"And friend Harsek, here?" I asked. "What function does he perform?"

Priscilla smiled. "Why, he is the communist menace against whom we, as Mr. Leonard's operatives, have been struggling. There had to be some obvious and conspicuous adversary, did there not? If there had been no visible enemy, even Mr. Leonard, stupid as he is, might eventually have begun to wonder suspiciously why things were forever going wrong with his brilliant plans. But with the great Harsek opposing us, we raw U.S. recruits could be excused for a few failures—the great Harsek and the equally well-known Vadya."

"I see," I said. "Very ingenious."

Priscilla said, "Of course, where Vadya was concerned, there was a further motive: the people back home had been somewhat concerned about Vadya lately. Her continuing relationship with a certain U.S. agent had caused a few doubts about her reliability. We were asked to investigate. We found the doubts to be justified and took action accordingly—first selling it to Mr. Leonard, of course, as necessary retaliation for her murder of one of his agents in Acapulco. We persuaded him that his 'image'—a word he loves—that his image and that of his agency would be forever tarnished if the woman were permitted to live, and he gave the appropriate orders."

I asked, "And just exactly what did Vadya do to justify those doubts of her reliability?"

Priscilla laughed maliciously. "Need you ask? Are you
going to pretend, at this late date, that there was nothing
between you? I saw the way you greeted each other,
remember? I was following when she took you for a cozy
evening tour of Mazatlán, including… including a certain
area that should not have been called to your attention.
I saw you afterwards speaking together very seriously
in the restaurant where you had dinner, the place with
the odd name: The Glass of Milk. Obviously she was
negotiating with you, her lover, for sanctuary in the
United States. What was she offering and what price did
she ask?" Priscilla shrugged. "It does not matter. I saw
enough to confirm that she had to be eliminated. I had
already made the arrangements; one likes to be prepared.
It was only a question of carrying them out."

I felt Carol stir uneasily beside me, listening to these
details of my secret life, but for the moment she didn't
count. I was thinking of another woman I'd known, and
of the fact that there are always people, on both sides,
who have a thing about fraternizing with the enemy, even
when it's done with the most patriotic motives. So Vadya,
without a thought of betraying her country, had died at the
hands of her own people because a vicious, suspicious girl
had misconstrued her behavior. Well, it wasn't exactly a
new idea. The possibility had occurred to me before, when
I'd had time to think about what had happened.

Harsek spoke suddenly: "There is the island, below us.
And there is the boat, on schedule."

I looked down and saw the crescent-shaped island

below, and a black power cruiser of reasonable size, the kind with a cockpit large enough to hold a couple of fishing chairs.

Harsek was still speaking: "Have no fear, Mrs. Lujan. You will be picked up almost before you have time to get wet."

He was a little too reassuring, a little too soothing; and Priscilla was watching me too closely. There was something in her eyes that I did not understand; I could think of no personal, private reason for her to show so much hatred and triumph. Between agents, even agents of hostile nations, it was an unprofessional display of emotion.

She said, "Of course, it was not expected that Laura would die because of your trigger-happy behavior. I am not forgetting that, Helm! You killed her and you will pay for it. Very soon now you will pay!"

She was quite a pretty girl, but I saw again the funny dry look in her face that I'd once taken for unawakened virginity, but which I now realized was something quite different. I remembered a red-haired girl saying casually: *come to that, I'm not really sure she likes boys.* If true, it explained a number of things about Priscilla Decker, including the fact that her sexy getup had never seemed quite convincing, even when she was presumably luring me to her room for purposes of seduction.

It also explained the cold hatred in her eyes; and I realized suddenly that all this business of life-jackets and ditching-advice meant nothing where Carol and I were concerned, because we were not intended ever to leave the cabin. We were merely being kept docile and unresisting until the time came to slam the door in our faces—to the accompaniment of a few shots if necessary—and let us sink with the plane.

After all, we served no useful purpose. We'd merely been brought along because there had not been time to dispose of us neatly, earlier. Well, it was too bad. I'd hoped to get farther and learn more, but obviously this was, for the moment, the end of the line. Somehow I'd have to find another streetcar to take me the rest of the way.

I looked at the girl in the front seat, and gave a malicious laugh. "Sure," I said deliberately. "Sure, I killed her. But what's one bull dyke between friends? You can find another soon enough."

I heard Carol gasp at my crudity—I was getting a little tired of that mechanical ingenue reaction—but I was really watching Priscilla, waiting for her response, and it came. Her face went totally white, her eyes narrowed dangerously, and her finger tightened on the trigger.

I yelled loudly, as if giving a prearranged signal: "All right, Carol! *Now!*"

Priscilla's eyes wavered for an instant, giving me time to grab the gun and force it aside before it fired. The crash was very loud inside the cramped cabin.

Harsek did not move for a second or two. The bullet hole in the right side of his neck was clean and small, but the exit hole on the left side was ragged and much bigger, and there was blood and stuff splattered all over the window beside him.

Then he slumped forward against the controls, and the plane nosed down in a screaming dive towards the Sea of Cortez, five thousand feet below...

20

I had not, of course, intended for anything of the sort to happen. In fact, I would have been happy to remain a model prisoner as long as the plane was in the air. As I have indicated, they kind of scare me. On the other hand, the idea of plumbing the depths of the Gulf of California trapped inside a winged plexiglass-and-metal coffin scared me even more.

My spur-of-the-moment plan, if you could call it that, had merely involved distracting and disarming Priscilla while Harsek had his hands full with the plane, and then coming to terms with the Mad Czech somehow. It wouldn't have been easy, since a man at the controls of an aircraft has certain advantages over a passenger with a pistol he's obviously not going to shoot unless he wants to commit suicide for everybody on board. But it had seemed worth trying. However, when you start wrestling for firearms in a confined space, anything can happen...

The plane was still heading downwards at a considerable

angle and steadily increasing speed. My impulse was to strap my seat belt tighter, close my eyes, and pray for heavenly intervention, but this seemed impractical, since my praying experience has been very limited, and some truly expert praying was obviously required here, if anything was to be accomplished that way.

I remembered reading, or being told, that modern light planes are pretty good at flying themselves out of trouble if you give them a chance. I drew a long breath, unfastened my belt, leaned forward, and pulled the dead man back into his seat.

Carol was clutching at my coat and making some panicky noises, to which I paid no attention. I'd already determined that she couldn't fly. Priscilla, bracing herself stiff-armed between the seat and the instrument panel, was staring at Harsek wide-eyed and shocked, as if waiting for him to come back to life and take over again.

It was fairly obvious that she didn't know what to do or she'd have started doing it already, but I shouted: "Can you fly?"

Her face turned towards me. "What?"

"Can you handle this plane?"

She shook her head convulsively. "No. No, of course not. Can't you? My God, what are we going to do?"

Still hugging Harsek with one arm, I turned the gun around and shot her. She stared at me blankly, uncomprehending. Then she died and fell back against the right hand door. I thought that was rather nice of her. At least she'd had the decency to stay off the controls.

Carol was yanking at me again. "Matt, have you gone utterly *mad*—"

I was studying the instrument panel for inspiration. I'd seen quite a few of them on one job and another, and I'd whiled away the long hours of various secret flights trying to figure out which dial meant what; sometimes I'd even asked a silly question or two. Now was obviously the time to fuse all those scattered scraps of aeronautical information into real understanding.

"Matt—"

I said without turning my head: "Get her out of here."

"What?"

"You heard me," I snapped. "Open the door and dump her. Then give me a hand with this one—"

"But you *shot* her!"

I looked aside irritably. "For God's sake, Carol! We've got a dead man and an out-of-control airplane on our hands! Do you want us to keep a dangerous enemy agent around for a pet, as well? Sure I shot her. What else could I do with her? If I hadn't, she'd have loused us up the minute she stopped being scared, and I'd most likely have been too busy to stop her. Now, for the love of Christ, let's dump the stiffs so I can maybe do something with this berserk machine before it flies us straight into the drink!"

There followed a rather ghoulish performance that had some elements of what I think is known as black comedy. The door of an airplane traveling at well over a hundred miles per hour doesn't open easily, and a dead body isn't very maneuverable under the best of circumstances. I had to leave Harsek to give Carol a hand, and even then we might not have made it if the plane hadn't obligingly executed a kind of sideways flip that released the air pressure for a moment, almost dumping out live and dead indiscriminately. I hauled Carol back inside and latched the door.

"That's enough of that!" I panted. "One down and one to go. Climb up front there and give me some room." I helped her over the seats. "Good girl! Now we'll snake this one back here instead of trying to… What's the matter?"

Carol was staring at her hands, which had blood on them. It happens when you're dealing with bodies freshly dead of gunshot wounds, but apparently this hadn't occurred to her until now. Her glance shifted, horror-struck, from the blood on her hands to the smears on her sweater and life-jacket. Her face turned a pale greenish color. She gulped and looked at Harsek in a sick way.

"I… I can't. Matt, I just can't bear to touch him!"

Sometimes I have serious doubts that nice girls are here to stay. They're delightful to have around in times of noncrisis, but their survival value is open to question. They always seem to have some sentimental or fastidious reason for not doing whatever's necessary to keep on living. I found myself remembering my former wife, another nice girl who'd been a total loss when things got messy.

I said sharply, "Snap out of it! You can puke later, Angel. Right now, just grab hold of the bloody cadaver, bravely and firmly, and give it a boost aft so I can get to those controls!"

It worked. It angered her enough so that she forgot her incipient nausea, temporarily at least; and a moment later I was in the driver's seat, for whatever good it might do me. My surroundings looked, in some respects, like rush hour at the butcher shop, but that was irrelevant.

What was important was that the plane's nose was down again and I was looking through the windshield at water ahead, close enough that I could see detail in the white crests of the waves. The altimeter read less than a thousand feet, dropping. I took hold of the gadget between my knees and pulled it towards me. The plane immediately made a surging, roller coaster rush skyward, and started to fall over on its side.

I hastily shoved the stick or yoke or whatever they call it back where it had been and let go of it. The motors were laboring uncertainly. I started to reach for the throttles and pulled my hand back: I didn't really know whether we needed more power or less. The plane was flopping around in the sky like a wounded duck, but I left it alone, and presently it straightened itself out and started flying in a more reasonable manner. I took hold of the controls again, this time using only thumbs and forefingers, very gently; and I drew the thing back to me a delicate fraction of an inch at a time...

The important thing, obviously, was to get the damn bird a safe distance up into the sky so I'd have a little room to make mistakes in. Gradually, I got things sorted out after a fashion—rudder, elevator, ailerons and the works.

The altimeter began to show a profit instead of a loss.

I was actually flying the machine, more or less, or it was flying me. Anyway, it began to look as if we might remain airborne for a while, and it was time to decide what to do next.

I looked around. It was full daylight now, and for a startled moment I could see nothing but water below. I had a panicky feeling we might be lost out over the Pacific, heading for China, or rather, since we still seemed to be aimed generally southwards, South America and the Antarctic. Then I saw some shadowy dots of land far behind on the right quarter. The next project, obviously, was to get our flying machine headed back that way.

It took some experimentation since a plane, I quickly learned, can't just be steered where you want it to go, it's got to be banked as well. Furthermore, the rudder pedals worked backwards from the way they had on the Flexible Flyer racing sled I'd used as a boy—a detail that tended to confuse me in moments of stress.

At last we were headed kind of northwest, however, and I discovered some knobs and cranks—the ones Harsek had used right after takeoff—that let me adjust things so the aircraft was flying itself without my heavy-handed guidance. Early during all these efforts, I had been aware of my passenger being violently ill, but there had been nothing I could do about it, so I'd left her to her own devices. Now she spoke, steadily enough but a little apologetically:

"Aren't you… aren't you steering the wrong way, Matt? The mainland is east of us, isn't it? Shouldn't we be heading into the sun, rather than away from it?"

I said, "I've lost nothing on the mainland, doll. I'm looking for a crescent-shaped island and a boat about forty feet long."

"But—"

I sighed patiently. "Carol, we came on this ride to learn something, didn't we? At least I did. There's a place I'm supposed to find. You heard the girl. Something's planned for the next day or two. A flaming horror, a mass catastrophe connected with this flying saucer hoax, she indicated, to be framed on the U.S. I've got to know where."

"But she's dead and so is the man—"

"The people on that boat aren't dead, are they? If I can get us down somewhere near them, they'll take us aboard, if only to find out what happened up here. And then, presumably, they'll head for wherever the action is to be, and that's the place I want to go." I made a wry face. "Priscilla gave me a hint, but it was only a hint. I can't afford to gamble when there's a chance of making sure."

"Sure? What's sure about it? You don't know how to land an airplane, do you? You've got to find an airport; you've got to have somebody telling you—"

"In Spanish?" I said. "How many flying terms do I know in Spanish? How many do I know in English? Hell, I'd fly us into the ground while I was trying to figure out what the guy was saying. Anyway, I'm doing all right for an instant aviator, aren't I? I'll get us down somehow."

"And what if you kill us? How sure is that?" She drew a long breath. "Oh, all right, darling. I suppose you have to try. What can I do to help?"

I glanced at her. I guess I'd forgotten that while nice girls often have weak stomachs, there's generally nothing fundamentally wrong with their courage. She gave me a funny, wry little smile as if she knew exactly what I was thinking.

"I… I'm sorry I disgraced myself," she said. "I'm not used to blood, Matt."

"Sure."

"Tell me what to do."

I shrugged. "Since you ask, our friend in back should have at least three guns on him: a Luger, a Browning, and another pocket pistol belonging to our friend Solana. Priscilla handed them over to him, back there on the highway. Get them, and then strap him in. I'll get us down, but I won't say how. He's a big guy and we don't want him to come flying through the cabin when we hit."

Carol winced. "You have the most untactful way of putting things of any man I've known. It would serve you right if I sicked up all over you!" She turned around, kneeling on the seat. "Here's your arsenal. Where do you want it?"

I took the guns and looked at them. The plane was flying along docilely, no hands, at three thousand feet and a hundred and forty miles per hour. I could afford to take my attention off it for a little. I looked at the big, slim-barreled Luger with which Harsek had made his reputation, checked the loads, and dropped it into the coat pocket that already held Priscilla's Colt .38. I glanced at the compact Browning I'd taken from Vadya's purse, it seemed a long time ago. I rechecked that, since it had been out of my possession, and put it in the other coat pocket. I hefted Solana's very similar automatic and started to dispose of it the same way, but stopped, frowning.

For a gun almost identical to the Browning, it had a startlingly different balance. Well, that happens. Take two shotguns of the same general type and weight but different manufacture, and one will feel light and alive while the other feels heavy and dead, depending on how the weight is distributed. The same can be true of pistols, if you've had experience enough to recognize it in the smaller weapons. But here the difference was so marked that a little investigation seemed indicated.

I removed the clip. It appeared to be fully loaded. I jacked the remaining cartridge out of the chamber, and it seemed to be an ordinary .380 round. I picked up the clip again, to reload, and realized belatedly that it was much too light for the five or six cartridges it was supposed to hold.

Studying it, I began to laugh. It was a very simple arrangement. There was a perfectly good cartridge in the chamber, and another in the top of the clip, so the gun would fire two shots just like any other gun. It would seem fully loaded to anyone who made a routine check. However, the lower part of the clip held no cartridges, although it was carefully camouflaged to show a gleam of brass wherever it was supposed to. I thought I had a pretty good idea of what was inside it, and it wasn't powder and lead.

"What is it?" Carol asked. "What's the matter with it? What's so funny?"

I grinned. "Our friend Solana's simpleminded plot wasn't quite as simpleminded as it seemed. Here's his real tracking device. The one you were carrying was just fool-bait."

She flushed. "Well, I think that's… kind of disgusting! You mean that whole act he had us go through was… wasn't really supposed to convince anybody?"

"Well, Priscilla was obviously supposed to see through it. She was supposed to search you, and find that gadget in your boot, and relax. And all the time the real beeper was in the gun. Solana knew no pro would leave a loaded gun behind." I laughed again. "Not bad! Hell, I could get real fond of that tricky little greaser!"

"Matt!" Carol had all the usual nice-girl horror of derogatory racial terms.

"He called us *gringos*, why can't I call him a greaser? In an affectionate way, of course. But I'll call him a clever Castilian gentleman if you prefer. Anyway, that should mean we're not alone up here." I looked around at the blue morning sky. "There must be a plane up there somewhere, tracking us. Well, let's hope the pilot is on the job." I looked down at the half-dismantled weapon in my hand, and began to reassemble it. "It means, also, that I've got to change my plans a bit. I've got to figure out how to get this damn electronic firearm into enemy hands under very convincing circumstances, preferably without getting shot in the process—"

"Matt, look! There's a boat down there, heading this way. And there, off to the right, is an island shaped like a new moon. Is that the one you wanted?"

It was the island, all right, but saying that I wanted it was putting things a little too strongly. Now I had to live up to my brave words and get us down somehow, preferably alive.

21

As we passed over the black power boat, it was swinging around to follow us back towards the island. Obviously it had headed off to chase the plane when it appeared to be in trouble. Now the boat was out of position for the pickup, which could be good or bad, depending on how things worked out.

If I managed to land us in one piece, I would be happy to have a little breathing space before the opposition arrived. On the other hand, if I cracked us up badly, it would be nice to have somebody—anybody—standing by to haul us out of the wreckage before it sank.

There were three men visible on deck, looking up. That meant a probable total of four, I reflected, figuring one steering. Of course there could be another at the radio, trying to make contact with us. In fact, the boat could be crammed with concealed, hostile manpower like a Barbary pirate, but it was hard to see what the point would be. A crew of four seemed like a reasonable working assumption.

They were having it rough down there, I saw, hammering into the big seas as they turned, with spray flying high. We passed over them at several times their speed, steady and comfortable, proving, I guess, that there's something to be said for progress.

I dismissed them from mind, temporarily, and concentrated on the island coming up ahead. There had to be something good about that island; Harsek had presumably picked it carefully. It was undoubtedly far enough from civilization that there was no chance of having some public-spirited Mexican citizen report seeing a plane go down into the drink; but it was also, presumably, a safe place to ditch with the wind in this direction. Well, I hoped the Czech had made a good choice, because I was stuck with it.

One of my few authenticated pieces of aeronautical information said that a plane must land into the wind. I lined things up carefully, therefore, while I was still several miles out. No windsocks were available, of course, but the waves below served just as well. At least I hoped they did.

When the island was dead upwind from us, I made a cautious, clumsy turn and headed in, gradually throttling back the motors and shedding altitude—so gradually that we were still some eight hundred feet up when we passed over the target area. Well, it wasn't a bad idea to take a look at what I was getting myself into, I told myself.

Two slim, curving, sandy promontories formed the outer ends of the scrap of land below. The center was wider and rose, I estimated, to some twenty or thirty feet above sea level. It looked pretty barren. There were hints of stuff growing here and there, but it wasn't a tropical garden by any means, just an overgrown sandbar, with a couple of lumps in the middle. You could call it a fat new moon, or you could call it a skinny crab with claws embracing a sheltered bay or lagoon. Obviously I was supposed to come gliding in between the claws and make my splash in the calm water beyond.

I made another of my shaky turns and headed back downwind, taking the time as we passed the island, just to be systematic. I gave us a good two minutes, and made another one-eighty. This time, after getting lined up properly, I pulled the throttles back more decisively, letting the speed drop significantly as we headed back in, descending.

The airspeed indicator said we were going slower, but the water seemed to go by much faster as we neared it. Suddenly the entrance to the bay was flashing past and we were still much too fast and much too high. I had a momentary, suicidal impulse to shove the controls hard forward and dive her in and get it over with; then I put on full power instead, and climbed out of there.

When I had enough altitude to feel safe—well, moderately safe—I made my downwind turn again. At least I was getting that technique under control. Four or five miles out, by my watch, I turned again, like an expert.

"Okay," I said aloud. "That's enough practice. Hold your hat, we're going in."

I didn't look at Carol as I said it. She was a smart girl;

I probably wasn't kidding her a bit. This time I forced myself to put it down faster and run the throttles back even farther—so far that suddenly I realized we weren't going to make it. The airspeed was dropping fast; the controls were getting heavy and unresponsive; and the island was still a good mile ahead. The big, white-capped waves were reaching up for us, and if we hit here, away from the shelter of land, the plane would probably break up and sink too fast for us to get clear, assuming that we lived through the impact...

I started to reach for the throttles once more, and drew my hand back. To hell with it. There are times when you can repair your mistakes, but there are also times when you'd damn well better just live with them. If I started to horse around now, at this low altitude and sluggish speed, I'd probably lose control altogether and make the crash worse. I concentrated on keeping the damn bird straight and level as it sank towards the water. Anyway, my line was good, and every second brought us closer to the entrance.

Suddenly the two horns of the crescent were welcoming us, and I realized that, far from hitting short, we were probably going to overshoot and crash into the island. I reached out and cut the ignition switches and flipped a mental coin. It seemed better—or at least slower—to flop in tail first than to dive in. I yanked the controls brutally back into my lap. All kinds of things happened at once. The nose went up, the right wing dropped, the tail hit the water, and the whole plane came crashing down on its belly, hard. The low wing dug in, and we went plowing blindly across the lagoon.

Then everything was very quiet, and we lay there rocking gently, with water draining from the windows and windshield. I looked at Carol, who lifted her head and looked at me.

I grinned. "A good landing is any landing you can walk away from—as we birdmen say."

"Walk?" she said shakily. "Swim, you mean. Let's get out of here!"

She unbuckled her seat belt. The door opened easily, which was a relief; I'd had a sudden fear that it might have jammed somehow. Then she was out of there, and I was scrambling after her, but I stopped for a moment to look around. After all, there was some sentiment involved: this was my first aircraft command. Now that it was over, I realized that it had been kind of fun driving the thing around the sky.

I looked at Harsek, huddled behind the seats, and felt less happy. It was a hell of a way for an experienced agent to go, shot by accident while acting as window-dressing for an operation being conducted by some vicious kids with odd sexual appetites. Harsek, the Mad Czech. I wondered how he'd come by the name; he'd seemed sane enough to me. Well, as sane as they come in this racket.

I wondered if, perhaps, as in Vadya's case, there hadn't been a little more to Harsek's story than we'd been told. Perhaps somebody'd had some doubts about him, too, to send him here in a subordinate capacity. Maybe he'd been disciplined for making an error of some kind during the recent Mid-Eastern disturbances…

"Matt!" It was Carol's voice. "Matt, hurry, it's sinking!"

I gave Harsek a salute, as one pro to another, and squeezed my six-feet-four out through the door. Carol, her life preserver inflated, was crouching on the half-submerged wing. I paused to yank the tab, and felt my rubber vest fill, which was just as well. With all the firearms in my pockets, I'd have sunk like a rock without the extra buoyancy. I looked out to sea and saw that the black power cruiser was only a mile or so out, heading straight for the entrance.

The plane was settling fast. I sat down and slid into the water, which was warmer than I'd expected. Carol hesitated a moment longer, conventionally reluctant to go swimming fully dressed. Then the plane gave a sudden lurch, and she launched herself cautiously, being careful to keep her head above water. She glanced in my direction to make sure I was coming, and started making her way towards shore in an embarrassed, gingerly manner, as if afraid her friends might see her paddling around in the Pacific—well, an arm of it, anyway—with all her clothes on.

It wasn't much of a swim. Five minutes later we were wading up to the beach.

22

Flying might be fun, and swimming was all right in its place, but dry land felt very good to me as I peeled off my life-jacket and tucked my wet shirt into my dripping pants. Even a lonely sandspit in the desolate Gulf of California had a lot to recommend it.

I looked at Carol and grinned. She'd made it ashore without getting wet above the neck, and her smooth blonde hair, only slightly windblown, looked ridiculously neat and civilized above her sagging sweater and wetly clinging skirt.

I said, "Ditch your waterwings and let's go."

"Go where?" She tossed the inflated vest aside, and bent over to pull the brief safari skirt away from her legs. Wringing it out by sections, she looked around the isle, and glanced at the approaching boat. "There's no place to hide, Matt. The whole island's only a mile or so long and a few hundred yards across, mostly sand. They're bound to catch us."

"Sure," I said. "But let's dress it up a bit and make it look impressive. I'd like to find a picturesque spot for Helm's Last Stand, over towards the middle there. The lower of those two sandhills, I think, so they can show their tactical genius by eventually outflanking us from the other one. We'll hold them off bravely, though, until death stares us in the face. Can you shoot a pistol?"

"No. Matt, I—"

"So much the better. They've got to be healthy to show us the way, so we don't really want to hurt them. Well, maybe just one, to make it look good. Three can handle the boat and prisoners. But by God we'll go down with a bang. A lot of bangs." I patted my weighted pockets. "They'll think they've fought the Battle of the Bulge before they capture and disarm us."

"Matt, be serious. If you start a lot of shooting… Well, they'll shoot back, won't they? I don't think I'm a coward, but I don't particularly want to get killed just so you can make a dramatic gesture."

I said, "Don't run down dramatic gestures, doll. Dramatic gestures are absolutely essential in this business." I hesitated, and glanced at her. I still had my orders, but the situation had changed somewhat, and I said, "I will now make a confession. I really am a secret agent of sorts. Just don't tell anybody I told you, particularly my boss."

Carol smiled faintly. "Well, I'd kind of begun to suspect it."

"I even have a bit of a reputation in my line of work,"

I said modestly. "In fact, I have a dossier as long as your arm in certain people's files. What I'm trying to say in my diffident way is, I'm known from here to Moscow—and maybe even to Peking—as a hotshot spook, smart as a fox, dangerous as a wounded grizzly. At least I hope I am. Whether the reputation is deserved or not is beside the point. The fact is, I'm just not supposed to be the kind of guy you'd find sitting on a sandbar with folded arms, waiting to be taken prisoner."

"But, Matt—"

"Let me finish. The message I am trying to convey is that if whoever's on that boat catches me too easily, he'll know it's a trick. He'll poke and pry and ask questions, trying to discover why I'm playing mouse. He may even take a good look at the weapons he's captured with me; the weapons I was so uncharacteristically reluctant to use. We wouldn't want that, would we? Friend Solana's trick pistol has come this far unsuspected. Let's try to make sure it completes the journey—even if we don't."

There was a little silence. Carol leaned against me to slip off her boots and empty them. For such fashionable and relatively diminutive footgear, they held a lot of water. Only when she had finished did she speak, very quietly.

"What you're saying is that it doesn't really matter if we're killed, just so the pistol makes it."

I nodded. "Well, just so somebody makes it, in this case Solana. But the pistol is our contribution, as it works out. We'll have to take Solana's competence on faith. We'll have to assume that he can make it on his own, given the proper electronic guidance. He shouldn't have too bad a hangover from that stuff I gave him. I cut the dose pretty short. By now, he's been awake for hours."

"But you don't *really* know what's being planned, do you?" Carol looked at me soberly. "You don't *really* know that finding it and stopping it is… is important enough to die for, Matt."

I said, "Some people have put a lot of work and thought and time—months of time—into this flying-saucer buildup. Judging by the number of deaths they're already responsible for, what they're working up to must be pretty spectacular. And they've got hold of a good idea. As Priscilla pointed out, people aren't going to be rational about the evidence. Some, as she said, are going to believe in visitors from Alpha Centauri come hell or high water—but there are also lots of folks who are already convinced that the U.S. is covering up some big secret because of the bumbling way the Air Force has handled the whole UFO bit. Given a really gory Mexican saucer incident, presumably caused by secret American machines, piloted by conscienceless American flyers, and God knows what the international repercussions may be. We're already in trouble in Latin America; an incident like that could make it all go the way of Cuba. Certainly we won't come out of it smelling of roses, no matter how vigorously we deny everything. Hell, we've been denying everything connected with UFOs for years. Who's going to believe more of the same?" I shrugged. "But that's all kind of irrelevant, as far as I'm concerned."

"What do you mean?"

I said, "Deciding what's important and what isn't is not my job. The man said stop it, so I stop it. Or I do what I can to make sure it gets stopped by somebody, in this case Solana."

I took her by the arm and led her towards the wider part of the island. The cruiser was standing in through the entrance now. I could see the three men on deck looking towards us, and the fourth man inside the deckhouse looking ahead to make sure he didn't hit anything.

One of the three men in the open looked familiar: a young man with streaky blond hair. That figured. I'd never really bought the idea that Priscilla's pretty-boy sidekick, Tony Hartford, had died heroically trying to save me from Harsek in Mazatlán. The idea had seemed even less plausible when I'd learned they were all on the same team. Now it appeared that Tony hadn't died at all. Well, he wasn't the first agent to have a phony demise staged for him so he could drop out of sight.

I recalled that some questions had been raised about his sexual attitudes, too. Administratively speaking, I suppose it made sense: if you had a number of them on the payroll, you might be better off working them together, hoping they'd understand and tolerate each other. Not that Tony's love life made much difference here. I wasn't planning to go to bed with the guy.

"Matt."

I glanced towards Carol. She wasn't looking at me; she was just watching where she put her feet as we plowed through the sand and brush and beach grass.

"Yes?" I said.

"Maybe I owe you an apology." Her voice was low. "Maybe… maybe this work of yours isn't all just tricks and lies and… and shooting unarmed women in cold blood."

"What unarmed women?" I asked. "Priscilla still had that .22 derringer with one barrel loaded, and don't think she wouldn't have used it instantly when she saw her chance. And taking time out to disarm her wasn't exactly practical up there, if you recall the circumstances."

"Nevertheless, it was a pretty brutal thing you did, Matt. But… but if you're prepared to sacrifice your own life as readily as somebody else's, that does make you look a little better. Much better, in fact."

"Sure," I said sourly. "I'm a great patriot at heart, a silent soldier of the grim undercover war that never ends. Just pat me on the back and call me Horatius, Junior; the guy who holds the bright bridge of Freedom against the dark forces of Tyranny. Shit, if you'll pardon the expression."

She said stiffly, "I was trying to… to understand, darling."

"Well, you're not making much headway. How we look, to you or anybody else, is the least of our worries. But it occurs to me that while I'm pretty well constrained to be a patriotic hero right now, there's absolutely no reason for you to be a patriotic heroine. You've got no reputation to live up to. In fact, it might be better for everybody if you just break free right now—I'll hold on hard enough to make the struggle look good—and then run down there and wade out to meet them with your hands in the air. Tell them breathlessly that just because I'm a suicidal damn fool is no reason why you should—"

"Matt!"

"What's the matter now?" I asked.

Her expression was indignant. "You don't think much of me, do you? Just because I can't hold my lunch down after wrestling with a corpse, you think I'm a… a decorative little lightweight, or something."

I said, "You spend more time worrying about what you think of people and they think of you! This is not the spot to brood about appearances, sweetheart! You can't help me a damn bit by remaining faithfully at my side, so you might as well be sitting on that boat under guard, listening to the gunfire."

She said angrily, "Stop being chivalrous! You're not going to send me off to safety like a helpless child—"

I suppose it was very brave of her, but actually the idea of having her surrender independently had interesting possibilities. She might even carry Solana's automatic, and turn it over docilely, something Hartford would accept as natural from her but not from me. And however we worked the pistol deal, if I managed to get myself brought captive to the boat without being shot up too badly, it would be convenient to have an ally on board—an ally who wasn't quite as closely watched as I would be.

It was a promising gambit, but I could see that I wouldn't be able to use it, because she wouldn't buy it. Like most amateurs, she had a lot of screwball notions

about courage and loyalty, as if anybody gives a damn
how brave you are as long as your work gets done...

The boat was now passing the place where a wing-tip
and part of the tail assembly showed where the plane had
settled to the bottom, in water that was shallower than
I'd expected. Apparently I'd managed to drop us closer
to shore than intended by Harsek, who'd have wanted to
bury the debris deeply enough that it could not be seen.

Still holding Carol's arm, I started to run for the
higher ground ahead. I picked a nice spot in the dunes
overlooking the shore, and pulled out the big Luger,
the one weapon in my armory that might have some
effectiveness at long range.

"Lie down," I said to Carol. "Keep your head down.
Stick your fingers in your ears if you like. These toys are
kind of noisy."

I sat down on the edge of the hollow, dug my heels
firmly into the sand, and rested my elbows on my knees,
holding the Luger with both hands. It's a comfortable
weapon to hold but, because of the skinny, light barrel,
a hard one to hold steady. The boat slid past the plane
wreckage without pausing, aiming straight for the head
of the bay, and me. About thirty yards from shore, I saw
the propellers go into reverse. Hartford and his two pals
were up forward, preparing to jump. I counted two rifles
and one squirt-gun—submachinegun to you.

I waited until they were in the water; then I started to
peck at them with the Luger as they waded shorewards
holding their weapons high. They must have seen movies

of an amphibious operation somewhere, they had the assault style down pat.

My first shot was low. I saw the splash about halfway between the nearest man and shore. I let the front sight ride up in the rear sight notch and tried again, keeping my fire well away from Hartford. The fact that he was carrying the submachinegun kind of confirmed that he was in authority here, and I didn't want to lose him. He might be the only one of them who knew all I needed to find out.

My second shot either nicked the guy on the right, or came close enough that he changed his mind about going ashore. He turned, waving frantically for the boat, which was backing away. The man at the controls threw the engines ahead again. I put a bullet through his windshield but he was brave; he kept coming to the rescue of his embattled comrades. I threw a shot at the man on the left, missing by about three feet, but he didn't like the sound of it ricocheting off the water; he turned back, too.

Hartford was yelling at them angrily. He might be a fairy—although that wasn't proved—but he had guts enough to keep coming until it became obvious that he was also a general without an army. Then he stood there and gave me a burst from his weapon for effect, before he turned back and waded out and was hauled aboard the boat by his friends, who'd negotiated the cruiser's high bow faster than you'd believe it could be done. The steersman threw his engines into reverse again, and the boat slid back out of pistol range.

I said to Carol, "We'd better find a place to make

ourselves comfortable. Having tried a head-on assault and been driven back, the enemy will now regroup his forces and advance systematically from the flanks… There they go. One guy on the point to the right, two on the point to the left, converging towards the middle, us. That's what we call strategy, sweetheart. How do you feel?"

"Scared," she said frankly. She stood up, brushing at her clothes. "Do bullets always make that horrible screaming noise?"

"Wait till you hear one really close," I said. "That guy on the right, now. I feel he's superfluous. I don't want to have to watch him, sneaking up behind me. He's apt to shoot me in the back while I'm putting on my act for the other two. Let's pull back a little—there's a better foxhole up behind us—and you keep an eye on them. Here. Try an occasional shot with this .380; it doesn't kick much. Keep them under fire and tell me what they're doing while I get rid of this lone-wolf character…"

I built up his confidence, first. I used Priscilla's gun, which I had no faith in; it had too short a barrel for long-range accuracy, and she hadn't looked like the kind to be careful with her firearms, anyway. I was right, the .38 shot way low and left, but I managed to put them close enough that the guy knew he was being shot at, while still staying far enough away that he soon lost respect for my marksmanship. I heard Carol fire, and gasp.

"I thought you said this gun didn't kick!"

"Wait till you work up to a .44 Magnum," I said. "How are they doing?"

"They're taking it very slowly. I think they must want your man to get into position first."

"Well, he's coming right along," I said. "He's Sergeant York taking on the whole German army singlehanded. Ouch!" I ducked, as my man put a rifle bullet a couple of feet away, stinging my face with sand. "So my *amigo* knows how to shoot. That means he'd better not get much closer."

I fired the last shot in the .38 as the man darted from a clump of brush to the shelter of a dune. The bullet came only close enough to encourage him in the notion that he was invulnerable, at least to my lousy marksmanship. I dropped the revolver, and took out Harsek's big German automatic once more, and made myself a steady rest for my hands, lying there.

He came out of hiding fast, and dove for cover again after a weaving ten-yard sprint. I didn't shoot. This made him feel neglected, I guess, because after a little he looked out. I put the sights on him, taking a coarse bead to allow for the range, but I held my fire. He wasn't presenting quite enough target for a certain hit.

He slipped back into hiding, gathering himself for another dash; this time, however, overconfident, he ran straight when he emerged and not so fast. Maybe he was getting tired. I led him by roughly two feet and pressed the trigger of the Luger. He fell headlong and pushed himself to hands and knees. I took careful aim and fired again, and once more, and a third time. There was nothing to be gained by saving ammunition. After all, the guns should be pretty well empty when the time came to surrender—all the guns but one.

The man just stayed there on hands and knees, head down, unmoving. I was reaching back for the gun I'd lent to Carol when he finally collapsed and lay still. Well, no pistol has the instant knock-down power of a good rifle.

I said, "Okay here. How are your people coming?" I got no answer, and turned to see Carol staring at me, very pale. "What's the matter?" I asked.

"You… you *killed* him!"

"Wasn't that the idea?"

"But you deliberately kept shooting even after he was wounded! He was just crouching there, and you kept shooting!"

I looked at her and knew I'd done it at last. She'd forgiven the brutal murder in the sky, perhaps because of the harrowing circumstances, but this was too much for her sensitive nature to bear. It was all right, presumably, to kill a man with one powerful rifle shot, but to do the same thing with four feeble pistol shots was not to be tolerated.

I said, "Do we have to go into all that again, doll? Wounded men have been known to fire guns, but it has never happened with a dead man. I'm not going to get myself shot in the back by a guy I forgot to finish off, like a sentimental TV hero, or something. Okay?"

"No!" She licked her lips. "No, it's not okay! I—"

I was getting a bit fed up with her moral judgments, not to mention her incessant gasps of surprise or dismay. I said, "Damn it, if you don't like it, go out there and surrender like I told you in the first place… *Down!*"

I threw myself on top of her, as Tony Hartford opened up with his squirter from a nearby sandpile. The submachinegun burst threw sand all over us.

I said, "Goddamn all amateurs! You were supposed to be watching them, not me! Give me that Browning!"

I rolled to the side, and tossed some sand back at friend Tony with Vadya's .380. There was a man missing, and that worried me, but there wasn't anything I could do about it, pinned down by the rapid-fire weapon across the way. Then Carol screamed, and I saw a man aiming a rifle down at us from the knoll that was the highest point of the island.

I rolled aside again, and emptied the .380 fast enough to make him take cover temporarily. This gave us a chance to wriggle farther down into the hollow we occupied, but there was obviously nowhere to go from there, except into the path of somebody's bullet. Well, that was exactly the way I'd wanted it, wasn't it?

I looked at Vadya's empty automatic, and tossed it aside. I'd once had some notion of keeping it for a sentimental memento, or something, but it was a silly idea. I took out Solana's pistol, and glanced at Carol, huddled down beside me.

"Forgive the imprecations," I said. "Everything's working out fine, just fine. We hope."

Tony Hartford's voice called: "Helm!"

"Right here," I said. "Where would I be going?"

"I think you see the situation. If you raise your head,

my man will shoot it off. Throw out your gun."

I hesitated long enough to make it seem as if I were having a big struggle with myself. At last I called back, "It's empty. They're all empty."

"Toss them out anyway."

I reached for the Browning and lobbed it over the crest of the dune. I pitched the .38 Colt after it, and waited.

"Harsek carried a Luger," Hartford called. "Let's see it." I tossed out the Luger, and he said: "And one more."

He was trying it on for size; he couldn't know I had a fourth weapon. I let him wait some more. Then I picked up the Solana gun, kissed it once for good luck, and threw it after the rest. I heard sounds of movement on the other side of the dune.

"So they were all empty!" Hartford's voice said sarcastically. "Not a bullet in the lot—except for one automatic fully loaded! I ought to shoot you, Helm, just for that!"

I winked at Carol. Our electronic baby had found a home.

"All right," Hartford called, "all right, send the girl out." I nodded at Carol, and she got to her feet and walked out there, slipping in the sand. Hartford's voice came again: "Now you, Helm. Hands up, remember. Way up!"

I stuck my arms into the air and climbed over the ridge. Carol was standing in front of Hartford, looking small and disheveled and scared, with sand clinging to her soggy sweater and skirt. The rifleman was coming down the hill to join us. Hartford swung his ugly little squirt-gun to cover me.

I saw him smile slowly, and I knew he was going to shoot. I could hardly complain. It was the logical thing for him to do; it was exactly what I'd done to Priscilla, for exactly the same reasons. They were still valid. There was nothing he needed me for. Any questions he had to ask, he could ask Carol.

I was just a threat, a potential danger to him and his operation as long as I was alive. Any sensible man would kill me now, and young Hartford, whatever his real name was, whatever his sexual attitudes might be, undoubtedly prided himself on being eminently sensible.

I saw the submachinegun swing and steady, and I braced myself for a last-minute dive to somewhere, not that there was any hope of escape, but I might as well take it moving as standing still. Then there was a single sharp report from down near the shore, and Tony Hartford went to his knees and pitched forward on top of his weapon. The man with the rifle stopped and looked in the direction of the shot. He dropped his gun and raised his hands.

We turned to watch Señor Ramón Solana-Ruiz approach, accompanied by a couple of Mexican soldiers in khakis, one carrying a rifle with a telescopic sight.

23

"I am very sorry to have annoyed you by saving your life, Señor Helm," Ramón said in his stiff Mexican way. They insult very easily down there. "I will endeavor not to make the same mistake again."

I said, "Privately, I am very grateful, Señor Solana. Publicly, all I can say is, it's a hell of a sentimental way to run a secret service or whatever you're running." I walked over to Tony Hartford's body and retrieved the trick automatic. "Here's your gun back. I went to a lot of trouble to plant it on that guy, so it would lead you to the right place. I hope you have an alternative solution to our problem."

He took the pistol and glanced from it to me. "So that is what the fireworks were about."

"That's what."

"You are a brave man."

I said irritably, "Jesus Christ, what is this anyway, a mutual-admiration society? So I'm brave or stupid or something, who cares? And you're a great guy, too, and in spite of how wonderful we both are, we still don't know where the hell these people are going to pull off their big show, whatever it may be."

"We have this man, here, and the pilot of the boat. A little questioning—"

I said, with a glance at the lagoon, "You won't have the pilot long. He's making for the open sea at flank speed."

Ramón laughed. "Give me a little credit, friend. There's a patrol boat hidden behind the next island that can outrun him by ten knots. As for the rest, I could not have an American agent killed before my eyes. The reports I would have had to fill out would have interfered with my work for months. Besides, I had promised Mrs. Lujan that if she cooperated, she would be safe, and I was not sure how many people the man was going to shoot down, once he started. Those automatic weapons intoxicate some people." He glanced out to sea. "Here comes the patrol boat now. You see, the other boat is stopping to surrender. The pilot knows he cannot escape."

We watched the minor naval drama from the sandhill. Presently the two boats headed our way, bucking the sea that was still running. Below us, in the calm lagoon, even the underwater parts of the wrecked plane were dimly visible, from this height, through the clear water.

Carol said, "But how did you know where to come, Ramón?"

He shrugged. "It was a matter for the experts with the charts. With the help of the electronic device concealed in the pistol, we could trace the course of your plane and extrapolate—I believe that is the right word. We knew the approximate cruising range. Unless you changed course drastically at the last moment, you had to come down in the gulf within a certain area. Presumably there would be somebody to pick you up. A discreet radar search gave us the location of all vessels in the lower gulf. There is not much water traffic. It was not hard to pick out a fishing boat that was heading in roughly the right direction at top speed, and determine its course. Somewhere near the spot where the two courses intersected, there had to be a place suitable for either landing the plane or putting it down in the water. Our experts decided that this island was the most likely choice for an experienced pilot under the prevailing weather conditions. I made arrangements to conceal myself here with a couple of men before daybreak, sent the patrol boat off to hide, and here I am."

"We're really very grateful," Carol said. "No matter what Mr. Helm says."

"Of course he is perfectly right, señora. I did allow sentiment to interfere with duty. Now we must hope that these men will give the right answers under questioning."

"Assuming that they know them in the first place," I said grimly. "Maybe I can shortcut this inquisition a bit. It's a long gamble, but it may pay off."

Carol said quickly, "That's right, you said Priscilla had given you a hint—"

"The little girl with the big bosoms and the ready revolver?" Solana said. "I will be interested to learn what happened to her and the pilot of the plane. Later. What did she tell you, Helm?"

"Not much," I said. "Just that while their girl Vadya was showing me around Mazatlán, she apparently took me into an area she shouldn't have. Priscilla thought this was proof of Vadya's intention to betray everything to me. Of course it wasn't. Vadya wasn't the turncoat type. She just knew she was being watched—maybe she knew she'd be condemned no matter what she did—and it suited her sense of humor to tease the bloodhounds a bit. She certainly didn't say anything to make me think the place had any special significance, except that it wasn't the kind of place a woman would normally take a man on a romantic evening on the town. Viewing the sunset from Icebox Hill, okay; but watching a rusty freighter being loaded with seeds or grain or something wasn't likely to do much for the male libido."

"The docks?" Solana said. "In Mazatlán?"

I nodded. "I can't remember the name of the ship, if I ever saw it. But you'd better get on the air as fast as you can and check if it's still there…"

It was; and after all our efforts, the main part of the job got accomplished by the authorities in Mazatlán before we arrived, even though we made it across Cortez's Sea by boat and plane at speeds that would have curled old Hernando's hair.

Later that day, after conferring with his local counterparts in Mazatlán, Solana gave me the guided tour of the captured ship. The most spectacular part of the

exhibit was a concealed hold up forward that had been
fitted out as a kind of assembly line for the manufacture
of intriguingly scorched and crumpled scraps of flying
saucer—the kind of debris that might have got blown
around after such an unconventional aircraft had exploded
violently. As might have been predicted, a surprising
number of the scraps could be identified as being of U.S.
origin, one way or another.

I looked around the gloomy hold and grimaced. "You'd
think," I said, "that if they were going to all this trouble
and expense, they'd cook up a couple of real UFOs—I
mean actual flying models. I can see that the easiest and
cheapest way of spreading the rumors was to get a lot of
people to lie their heads off about what they'd seen; but
one or two honest-to-God saucers flying around would
have helped make the hoax more convincing."

Solana laughed. "Yes, that occurred to our friends, too.
The big trouble was—according to one of the prisoners
who has talked—that although they tried, they could not
make them fly. The saucer configuration is apparently
inherently unstable at any reasonably high speed, at least
as far as our technology is concerned. The Martians or
Venusians may be able to design such a craft to fly fast in
our atmosphere; we can't. At least, these people couldn't.
They had to be satisfied with the big lie."

I glanced towards the other side of the cavernous hold.
"What's over there?"

"Those are the fire bombs. And here are the maps that
show where in Mazatlán each bomb was to be planted,

and where each scrap of flying saucer debris was to be found. The day after tomorrow, after the city had gone up in flames, these remnants would have been clear evidence of American... Yes, what is it?" A man had come up. He spoke to Solana, who said impatiently: "Yes, yes, of course she is to be admitted. Yes, with her cameras. I gave the orders, did I not? She is to be given every assistance."

We waited, and in a moment Carol came in. She'd changed into a crisp, light, slacks-and-shirt outfit, and she was hung about with photographic equipment until she looked like a joke, but then, most pros do when they're working. It's only the occasional sensitive lone-wolf camera artist who can get by with interpreting the world about him, to his own satisfaction, with one camera and one lens. The guy who works for an editor's satisfaction generally needs all the gear he can drag around.

She said to Solana: "I certainly appreciate your having my stuff flown down, Ramón. Is it really all right if I take pictures in here?"

"In here, out there, everywhere," he said. "We want full coverage and as much publicity as we can get. When you are through here, you will be transported back to the island, if you wish, to get pictures there. But please be certain you first get some fine, sharp pictures of this UFO factory. For the sake of both our countries, the world must be convinced that this was all an elaborate fraud."

"Yes, of course." She made a little face. "That island isn't my favorite vacation spot, by any means, but you're right, we should have some shots of it. Can I get some of the people, too?"

"All you want, dead and alive, dear lady."

"Thank you." She was silent for a moment, and we all stood awkwardly in the middle of the iron room. Carol glanced at me and said, "Matt, I'm sorry if I said anything... I'm just not used to being involved in anything like that."

"Sure."

"I... I'll see you around."

I looked at her. She was telling me that it had been nice, this summer, but that was before she'd known what kind of man she was associating with: a coldblooded, ruthless, callous murderous type of guy dealing in guns and blood. Somehow, I found, it didn't quite break my heart. I'd got a bit disenchanted with her, too, during the course of our adventures. She was a nice girl—well, woman—and I hoped she'd find a nice boy—well, man— and in the meantime she had her cameras and her ideals and her notion of what the world ought to be like, even if it wasn't.

"Sure," I said. "Somewhere around."

Solana cleared his throat. "And me, señora? Will you see me around, too? I still owe you a promised dinner, if you recall."

Something odd and frightened showed in Carol's blue eyes for a moment. I realized she was trying very hard to act as if she were talking to two ordinary men, while the truth was that to her we weren't really men at all, now that she'd seen us in action. We were a different breed of animal, savage and vicious beasts of the dark jungle of espionage and intrigue that she didn't want to admit existed.

She licked her lips. "I… I'm sorry, Ramón."

"May one ask why?"

She hesitated. "I… I don't really know if I should… Well, all right. You remember the motel room in Puerto Peñasco, the one we watched from out on the beach that night? You let that poor man stay in that room, even though you knew he was going to be killed. All you cared about was learning which one of two people was going to shoot him. The fact that he was to die didn't concern you at all!"

After the silence had gone on for a while, I said, "I remember that poor man. That was the poor man who fed his wife a Mickey and burned her like a torch, wasn't it?"

Carol turned on me angrily and started to speak, but checked herself. There was still another awkward silence. Solana tapped me on the arm and jerked his head towards the door or hatch. I followed him out.

"Tell me one thing, friend," he said, outside. "You knew the little girl with the tight trousers was the one. How did you know?"

I grinned, trying to dismiss Carol's white face from my mind. Perhaps my heart had been broken a little, after all, just enough to make me want to hurt her slightly.

"How did you?" I asked.

Solana shrugged. "A man of experience learns to distinguish between passion and what is only a pale imitation of passion, *amigo*. That young lady was only an imitation sexpot, to use your Yankee term. She was not really interested in men. Her true interests obviously lay elsewhere. And perversion is a subject upon which your government is very sensitive. If the security of her department was so lax as to overlook her homosexual tendencies, what else had been overlooked?" He smiled faintly. "Besides, I was not impressed by her chief, when I met him. I do not trust stupid people, or people who work for stupid people. And then you did not shoot that murderer; she did. That confirmed it for me. Now tell me how you spotted her."

I said slowly, "There was a woman named Vadya, a communist agent, who walked into a room knowing that death was waiting inside. She was not a woman to give up easily. If the trap had been set by me, she'd have done her best to elude it or fight it. But there's a funny fatalistic streak in those people. Remember all those strange confessions in court many years ago? When I'd had time to think it over, I knew there could be only one reason why Vadya had walked into that room deliberately: because she knew her own side had pronounced the death sentence on her, and right or wrong she couldn't fight it. Which meant that the people who killed her had to be something other than the fine upstanding U.S. agents they seemed to be."

Solana nodded. "Well, it was a far-fetched plot, but it might have worked. I am not too fond of *americanos*, to be quite honest, but I do not want to waste my country's time and effort fighting them unnecessarily. Particularly if they are all as unpleasantly competent as you." He smiled. "But you really should learn how to fly an airplane, my friend. Watching you trying to bring that machine down was the most harrowing part of the whole assignment: I could not be sure you were not going to drop it right on my head. Now, is there anything I can do for you by way of showing gratitude?"

I said, "Well, you could save my life, but you've already done that. Do I still have some credit on the books?"

"Anything you like. What is mine is yours, as we say here in Mexico."

I said, "There was a girl with red hair who disappeared."

"We have her. She was in hiding aboard this ship, with several others. Or a prisoner. Apparently she was, herself, not quite sure which. She is guilty of the murders of three U.S. tourists and two Mexican nationals—the captain and the mate—who died when a fishing boat burned and sank, fired by a device planted by her. Afterwards she told a rather elaborate and convincing flying saucer story to explain the disaster. Do you want her?"

"Yes. I'll have to call Washington first, but I think we want her."

He shrugged. "I will not ask why. She is yours. As far as we are concerned, she will cease to exist. We have enough awkward cases to deal with, without hers."

I called Mac from the docks on a phone that Solana made available to me, and brought him up to date, I thought, only to find that he'd already got most of the information from other sources. He had some interesting news from the home front: the shining new agency that had been going to revolutionize the nation's intelligence systems was in the throes of a security shake up it was not expected to survive, and Herbert Leonard had been kicked upstairs to a fancy-sounding position with "coordinator" in the title. In Washington, whenever they start coordinating, they're pretty well through.

I said, "Well, I hope they don't start investigating us, sir, because I'm afraid I've been a little lax, security-wise."

"I gave you strict orders—"

"Yes, sir," I said. "But death was staring us in the face, and I needed the lady's understanding, and I figured that under the circumstances Leonard wasn't going to be worrying about anybody's security but his own."

"That is absolutely no excuse, Eric."

"No, sir. But after a couple of days of making a damn fool of myself playing the perfect clam, while everybody else was telling everything to everybody, my resistance just went down the drain, so to speak. Shall I send in my resignation, sir?" He didn't answer, and I went on: "If not, I have a suggestion to make…"

24

Annette O'Leary was waiting in my room at the hotel when I got there. She didn't look like a fugitive who'd been hiding out, or imprisoned, aboard a rusty freighter. Her long red hair was smooth and glossy, held by a black velvet band. She was wearing a short, slender, sleeveless black dress over which floated a sheer black garment known, I believe, as a cage—I sometimes wonder who dreams up these fashionable terms.

The filmy overdress, and her slim, high heels, gave her a fragile, ethereal look. Her suitcase lay open on the bed. There were wet towels strewn around the bathroom. Obviously she'd made good use of the facilities as soon as the police had brought her here. Well, she could have tried running away, instead. I would have been disappointed in her if she had.

"Ah," she said lightly, "the man with the ever-ready shower. And, I suppose, the handcuffs." She held out her wrists. "Take me away, officer. I'm guilty as hell."

I said, "That's no joke, O'Leary. They don't come any guiltier."

She sighed. "I might have known it was just a beautiful dream. Well, at least I got a bath out of it. Okay, which way is the jail?"

"Is that why you picked that dress, to go to jail in?"

"No, dad, I picked it to stay out of jail in, if I could. But I can see that you're not a bit impressed." She drew a long breath. "That's enough kidding, Mr. Helm. I'm not really in the mood. Why don't you just break down and tell me why you had me brought here."

I said, "You're a mass murderess, O'Leary. You killed five people—count them, five—just like snapping your fingers. Justice demands that you pay the supreme penalty, or spend the rest of your days in prison, regretting your crime."

She looked at me for a moment. Her greenish eyes were hard and bright in her small, freckled face. "And what am I supposed to do now, get on my knees and make with the remorse? Sure, I blew up the damn boat, and told a lot of far-out lies about what had happened out there. It was a stupid thing to do, and I did it for a stupid reason, but I was mad, and I don't think too clearly when I'm mad."

"What were you mad about?"

She said irritably, "You haven't done your homework, Mr. Secret Agent. My husband was killed, remember? They took him away and got him shot over in some crummy jungle or other. Was I supposed to keep loving the country that did that to him, and to me? So when some creep came up with some crazy plan for striking back I said, sure, I'll play. And I did. Like I say, I was mad."

"Are you mad now?"

"Not that mad," she said. "And now I know that I like foreign political creeps even less than the homegrown variety. There's nothing like playing footsie with a bunch of greasy conspirators to give a girl an acute attack of patriotism. But if you want me to say I'm sorry, to hell with you."

"Nobody wants you to say anything," I said. "And I mean that. Your remorse isn't wanted, but neither are your opinions on peace, war, or anything else. Can you keep your trap shut, O'Leary? You're no good to me if you're going to get mad and blow your stack all over again."

She was silent for a little while. Her tongue crept out and moved around her neatly lipsticked mouth, cautiously. "What do you want?" she asked at last.

"I have a new assignment coming up," I said. "For this assignment I need a good-looking, bloodthirsty, conscienceless little bitch who'll slit a man's throat and then kick him in the crotch for bleeding on her shoes."

Her eyes watched me steadily. "Well," she said, "well, I'm not very pretty, Helm."

"You'll do," I said. "You dress up pretty good. I'll pass you on the looks."

"Why… why me?"

I said, "Technically speaking, you did a nice, clean job on that boat. We like our people to be able to handle explosives. And your lies were good. The drunk act you put on for me was passable. For real professionalism, you need some training, but you've got the right attitude already, and that's half the battle. I don't see any black hollows under your eyes. You haven't been losing much sleep over those five innocent people who died because you got mad, have you? Morally, that's terrible, but we're not going to have much truck with morality, O'Leary, where we're going. That is, unless you'd rather go to prison."

She hesitated. After a moment, she turned away from me and walked to the door, and opened it. The wind fluttered her fragile dress and stirred her long hair. It was getting dark outside. The surf was beating against the beach just as it had the last time I'd been in Mazatlán. The offshore islands were black shapes against the dark sea and the darkening sky.

"You don't scare me," Netta said without turning her head. "You know that, don't you? You don't scare me one damn bit. If I take your crummy job, it won't be because of your crummy threats."

"Sure," I said. "What's the answer, or are you going to keep me in suspense?"

But I knew what her answer would be, because I knew what kind of a person she was, a person very much like myself. I saw her start to speak, but the words did not come. Instead she reached back quickly and grabbed my arm and held it, staring out to sea. I saw it now: something odd was happening over the dark shape of the islands. A pulsating green light was moving steadily and silently across the sky from north to south. We watched it until it disappeared over the town across the bay. The girl in front of me turned.

"Did you see it?" she breathed. "Did you *see* it? Why, it was a *real*—"

I said, "I didn't see anything, O'Leary, and neither did you. There's no such thing as a flying saucer. We've just proved conclusively that it's all a great big hoax, remember?" I grinned. "Besides, do you really have the nerve to tell another UFO story around Mazatlán?"

After a moment, she laughed and drew a long breath. "There's just one question, Matt," she said. "You said we'd have no truck with morality. Just how… just how immoral am I expected to get?"

I shrugged. "Just how immoral do you want to get?"

She smiled slowly, and took my arm again. "That's all right, then. Just so I have a choice."

We went back inside. I closed and locked the door behind us.

ABOUT THE AUTHOR

Donald Hamilton was the creator of secret agent Matt Helm, star of 27 novels that have sold more than 20 million copies worldwide.

Born in Sweden, he emigrated to the United States and studied at the University of Chicago. During the Second World War he served in the United States Naval Reserve, and in 1941 he married Kathleen Stick, with whom he had four children.

The first Matt Helm book, *Death of a Citizen*, was published in 1960 to great acclaim, and four of the subsequent novels were made into motion pictures. Hamilton was also the author of several outstanding stand-alone thrillers and westerns, including two novels adapted for the big screen as *The Big Country* and *The Violent Men*.

Donald Hamilton died in 2006.

ALSO AVAILABLE FROM TITAN BOOKS

PRAISE FOR DONALD HAMILTON

"Donald Hamilton has brought to the spy novel
the authentic hard realism of Dashiell Hammett;
and his stories are as compelling, and probably
as close to the sordid truth of espionage,
as any now being told."
Anthony Boucher, *The New York Times*

"This series by Donald Hamilton is the top-ranking
American secret agent fare, with its intelligent
protagonist and an author who consistently writes
in high style. Good writing, slick plotting and
stimulating characters, all tartly flavored with wit."
Book Week

"Matt Helm is as credible a man of violence as has
ever figured in the fiction of intrigue."
The New York Sunday Times

"Fast, tightly written, brutal, and very good…"
Milwaukee Journal

TITANBOOKS.COM

ALSO AVAILABLE FROM TITAN BOOKS

PRAISE FOR HELEN MACINNES

"The queen of spy writers." *Sunday Express*

"Definitely in the top class." *Daily Mail*

"The hallmarks of a MacInnes novel of suspense are as individual and as clearly stamped as a Hitchcock thriller." *The New York Times*

"She can hang her cloak and dagger right up there with Eric Ambler and Graham Greene." *Newsweek*

"More class than most adventure writers accumulate in a lifetime." *Chicago Daily News*

"A sophisticated thriller. The story builds up to an exciting climax." *Times Literary Supplement*

"An atmosphere that is ready to explode with tension… a wonderfully readable book." *The New Yorker*

TITANBOOKS.COM

ALSO AVAILABLE FROM TITAN BOOKS

PRAISE FOR DANIEL STASHOWER

"A romp that cleverly combines history and legend, taking a few liberties with each. Mr. Stashower has done his homework… This is charming… it might have amused Conan Doyle." *The New York Times*

"In his first mystery, Stashower paired Harry Houdini and Sherlock Holmes to marvelous effect." *Chicago Tribune*

"Stashower's clever adaptation of the Conan Doyle conventions—Holmes's uncanny powers of observation and of disguise, the scenes and customs of Victorian life—makes it fun to read. Descriptions and explanations of some of Houdini's astonishing magic routines add an extra dimension to this pleasant adventure." *Publishers Weekly*

TITANBOOKS.COM